DEATH BY DENIAL

For Sal –
with every
good wish
Peter Black
March '22
(and thanks for
the Amsterdam
adventure!)

Fiction by Peter Black

Seizure

Death by Denial

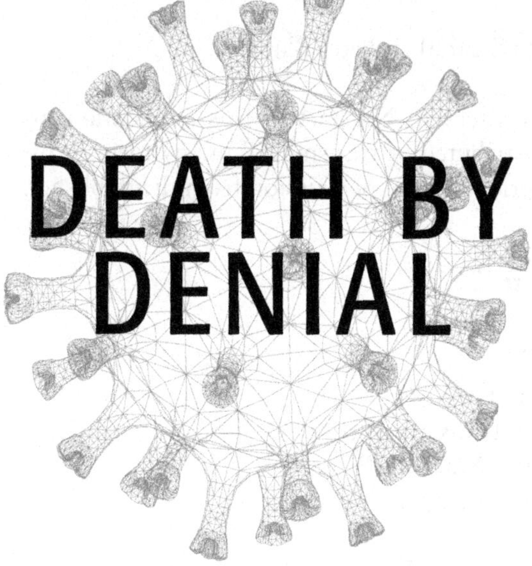

DEATH BY DENIAL

A Duncan MacGregor Novel

Peter Black

Skean Dhu Press
Cambridge, Massachusetts

Skean Dhu Press
1770 Massachusetts Avenue
Cambridge, Ma. 02139
Skeandhupress.com

Cover and text design by Mayapriya Long, Bookwrights
Printed in the United States of America

Death by Denial/PeterBlack.—1st ed.

ISBN 978-1-952683-03-9, paperback
ISBN 978-1-952683-04-6, hardbound
ISBN 978-1-952683-05-3, ebook

Dedicated to everyone who has had to deal
with Coronavirus:

Patients
Families
Health Care Providers
Essential Workers
Friends
All of us

CONTENTS

BAPTISM

CHAPTER ONE

ARRIVAL

MONDAY, DECEMBER 30, 2019
WUHAN, CHINA

Duncan MacGregor stepped out of the car. The stench of blood mingled with polluted air made him question his insistence on visiting the 'top Wuhan attraction' now in front of him.

Standing at the edge of Wuhan's live market, Mac watched vendors kill and eviscerate whole animals. Entrails and blood dripped from tables. Rabbit, bat, and chicken cages piled one on another. Urine and feces from one cage spilled over the one below, leaving stains on fur and running down to join the blood in the walkways. In the brittle cold of a winter morning, plaintive cries mingled with the incessant haggling of consumers and vendors.

Mac moved in toward the market.

"Please, no further," his host Wang Jin said, laying a hand on Mac's shoulder.

"It's not just the unsanitary conditions," Wang continued. "There are reports of a new pneumonia like SARS associated with this market. Don't—"

A police wagon screamed to a halt in front of them, stopping a cyclist pedaling furiously out of the market with a crate under one arm. Seeing the blockade, the rider jumped off his bike and slammed into Mac, jettisoning the box into the air. Shoppers screamed as whistles sounded shrill alarms.

Mac seized the man's arm and whipped him back toward the pursuing police. The crate splintered against the sidewalk, spilling its contents onto the street.

Onlookers scattered in a frenzy to catch what had been released. A few seconds later, a teenager lifted high an animal about fifteen inches long that looked like a cross between an armadillo and an anteater. Its scale-covered tail twitched as the creature torqued its armor-plated body to escape. The youth held firm. The crowd cheered.

"Are you OK?" Wang asked. "This is not how Wuhan people usually behave."

"I'm fine, but I should have listened to you in the first place," Mac said as he brushed himself off. "Can we move right on to the museum? There shouldn't be this much excitement around prehistoric skulls."

Once they were underway in the car, Mac asked, "What was the animal causing all the fuss back there?"

"A pangolin."

"A what?"

"A pangolin. A scaly anteater. Its meat is a delicacy, and

its scales are thought to have healing powers. The man was probably trying to sell it. That's against the law."

"So he'll go to jail?' Mac asked?

"Maybe worse, if that's what he had in the cage."

"Why?"

"Because he had close contact with pangolins. They carry the new virus I mentioned. He could already be infected."

"Is touching a pangolin the only way to catch the virus? Should I worry about the guy smashing into me back there?"

"We don't think one person can pass it to another. If that can happen, all Wuhan is in trouble."

"Not only Wuhan," Mac said. "The whole world could be in trouble, considering the way people travel these days."

CHAPTER TWO

MUSEUM, HOTEL, HOSPITAL

DECEMBER 30-31, 2019
WUHAN, CHINA

Duncan MacGregor knew skulls. Every day of his professional life, he sawed through them, repaired them, or discarded their fragments to let a damaged brain swell.

As his last stop of the day, he was eager to see the prehistoric skull specimens in the Hubei Provincial Museum.

Mac and Wang entered the exhibit room to find a group of teens clustered around the display case, blocking access to it. To Mac's horror, one of them raised a specimen off its pedestal. Laughing, the boy began to take a selfie, mocking the difference between his high forehead and the sloping forehead of *Yunxian man*. His companions cheered.

The clanging alarms deafened Mac, and the arrival of guards with semi-automatic weapons changed the tone quickly. The youth stood frozen with the specimen in his hand. A guard lifted it, put it back in the display case, then handcuffed the boy and led him away.

"Please remember not to touch the exhibits," Wang said.

"Wouldn't think of it," Mac replied, clasping his hands tightly behind his back. "I don't need any more excitement. Let's focus on what we have here. Am I right these 500,000-year-old human skulls did not come from our ancestors?"

"Correct," Wang said. "They're from *Homo erectus*. Populated the earth for 440,000 years before we came along."

"And we *Homo sapiens* killed them off?"

"Probably—or dominated them in other ways."

"How did we do that?"

"Maybe we were better looking?"

Mac laughed. "Possibly, but that's hard to tell from these specimens! I'm going to argue with you that it was our frontal lobes."

"How so?"

"Look how the forehead slopes almost straight back in these prehistoric skulls. *Yunxian man* had no frontal cortex. He could only follow instincts. We *Homo sapiens* have large frontal lobes under our high foreheads. Using them, we could develop science, strategy, and collaboration, which gave us a survival advantage over our enemies. We could reason and work together."

"I'm happy that you are still interested in such things, professor," Wang said with a grin that took Mac back to their time together in Boston. A tall, quiet Wang Jin had arrived as a postdoctoral fellow ten years ago, speaking only Mandarin. He had learned perfect English, developed into a skilled surgeon, and returned to Wuhan to become the youngest-ever chief of neurosurgery there. Still unmarried and completely dedicated to neurosurgery, Wang was now hosting Mac for five days as visiting professor.

"It's been a great day," Mac said as they left the exhibit. "This museum, the market, the Yellow Crane Tower, Mao Zedong's home, a dozen other Wuhan landmarks. But can we go to the hotel now?"

Mac's hotel, the Wanda Reign, sparkled like a diamond reflected in the water of the Yangtze River. Its lobby boasted a massive oval chandelier and marble floor, but Mac didn't pay much attention to them as he checked in and headed for his room.

He had only one objective—sleep. He unpacked, texted his wife Lauren that he was safely at the hotel, and went to bed.

The next morning, he lay for a few moments enjoying the crisp sheets before he flicked on WeChat video to connect with his family. He remembered Boston was twelve hours behind and caught Lauren, Maggie, and Peter in the middle of supper.

They began a lively discussion about time zones and the real date of New Year's Eve. Should it be based on the American date of January first, the Asian date based on the moon, or some different date Jewish or Muslim or other calendars prescribe?

Mac got so involved in the discussion he was late for the limousine scheduled to pick him up. He made it to the Zhongnan hospital five minutes before his lecture.

Wang met him in the hospital lobby with a cup of Starbucks coffee. They hustled to the auditorium and Mac began his presentation to an overflow audience. The need to wait until Wang translated each sentence slowed Mac at first, but after a few minutes he found a rhythm. Loud applause followed his final slide, and he answered questions at the front of the auditorium for an hour.

"I know we had planned a hospital tour today," Wang said after the last question was answered, "but the administrators have scheduled many meetings about this new virus. Can I leave you on your own until our official dinner tonight? The driver will pick you up at six."

Delighted to have the rest of the day to himself, Mac walked around the huge campus of Wuhan University, less than a mile from his hotel. He wandered among students and teachers, then hiked back to the Wanda Reign hotel. After lunch, he asked a hotel driver to take him to the Donghu Ecological Area. While the driver waited, he strolled through the magnificent park on the edge of the partly frozen East Lake. The temperature was just above freezing. Snow on tree branches added delightful ornamentation to the peaceful scene. He returned to the hotel refreshed, then showered and dressed for dinner.

During the limousine ride to the restaurant, Mac noted that Wuhan traffic was worse than New York. When he arrived at the Crane Palace restaurant, he found Wang at the entrance looking anxious. Mac and he ascended a staircase past two floors of diners, to a private room. A large circular table occupied most of the space, with twenty-four damask-covered chairs around it.

"Our guests will be right in. Don't eat too much at the beginning of the meal," Wang advised. "This is an official banquet, so there will be seventeen dishes. You'll be sitting beside the mayor and regional minister for health on one side. I'll be on your other to translate and the hospital director will be beside me."

After the guests arrived and seated themselves, Mac focused on food. There was brisk conversation around the table, but he could understand none of it. One woman directly across from him was particularly vocal. Her comments seemed to offend some of the others and at several points the discussion appeared explosive.

Wang named some of the obscure appetizers including sea urchin, eel, and octopus. Chicken, fish, and pork dishes with savory sauces and vegetable accompaniments were followed by fish maw soup. Rice, more hot dishes, and a dessert of fresh fruit and pastries finished the meal.

Mac found *baijiu*, the Chinese wine, especially difficult. Distilled from sorghum and millet, it tasted like turpentine and burned from his tongue to his midriff. As the guest of honor, he was obligated to drink many times in response to toasts from random fellow diners.

At the end of the meal, Wang tapped his water glass. "We are honored to have Professor Duncan MacGregor from Boston here as our visiting professor this year. He is a world leader in difficult brain tumor operations and global neurosurgery. Mr. Mayor, will you begin our speeches of welcome?"

The mayor, a jovial man in a dark suit, white shirt, and red tie, smiled at Mac. "Welcome," he said, raising Mac's hopes for a speech in English. Dashing them immediately, the mayor lapsed into Mandarin for fifteen minutes.

Neither the minister of health for Hubei province nor the director of the hospital even tried English. Wang translated furiously to keep up with them. After they finished, Mac had the opportunity to thank them all, with his brief remarks amplified and transmitted by his host.

The room cleared, senior officials first.

The woman who had been so vocal during the meal grabbed Mac's arm as he exited. She was about forty and appeared distraught, speaking in breathlessly accented English, "I am Dr. Chow Yuen, the head of the intensive care at Zhongnan Hospital. We have noticed something serious in the last two weeks. It looks like SARS, that respiratory virus that killed many of us in 2003." She looked around as if checking for spies. "I'm telling you because I hope you will use your influence to convince our hospital administrators to provide proper protective equipment for all of us. They just try to shut me up."

Mac saw Wang heading toward them.

"You'll see what I mean if you visit our ICU. Come by tomorrow," she said, and exited before Wang got to her.

"I see Dr. Chow has reached you," Wang said. "I assume she's discussing the new viral pneumonia I told you about. The hospital administration and local health authorities assure us it is under control. It's not much trouble yet, but we'll have to see. We don't quite know what we're dealing with. I hope she's wrong about what's happening. Sometimes her manner gets in the way of her message."

CHAPTER THREE

THE INTENSIVE CARE UNIT

WEDNESDAY, JANUARY 1, 2020
WUHAN, CHINA

Mac walked from the hotel to the hospital the next morning to celebrate New Year's Day. No ice had formed on the river, but the temperature still hovered around freezing. The sun tried without success to penetrate the smog. The wet air was irritating and pungent with smoke and ash.

Wang was again waiting in the Zhongnan hospital lobby. They maneuvered their way past families and patients who packed the entrance. In the pharmacy just to the left, hundreds of patients sat in plastic chairs waiting for their numbers to be called. On the other side of the lobby, the outpatient clinic had just as many patrons waiting to be seen by doctors.

"This is the best hospital in Wuhan," Wang said. "Thirty-three hundred beds, and a medical education center as well as a general hospital. The only Grade three Class A hospital in the city."

They ascended to the operating room floor and put on scrub clothes in the empty locker room. When they entered the neurosurgical operating suite, a sophisticated operating microscope sat like a star performer under the OR spotlight.

"Looks great. Do your people know how to use it?" Mac asked. He had seen hospitals where the fancy OR equipment remained a museum exhibit, never actually used in surgery.

"We use it every day, except these last few days. The same is true of our neurosurgical intensive care unit. It has thirty beds, but right now, it is—"

Dr. Chow headed toward them with a purposeful stride. "Ah, Dr. MacGregor. Let me show you the problem we discussed last night."

"Dr. MacGregor has a very tight schedule," Wang began. "I don't—"

"He should find time for this." Chow grabbed Mac's arm, propelling him through a set of double doors.

They moved into an ICU that looked like any Mac knew, except cloth drapes rather than walls separated patients. The beds were arranged in a circle around the central nursing station.

The wheezy inspiration and expiration of ventilators cycled continuously, with occasional pauses as nurses suctioned thick sputum from endotracheal tubes. The clanging of monitors, shouting of orders, and rustling of nurses and their assistants made a familiar sonic blend. The antiseptic used, however, had a different odor than Mac's familiar Harbor Hospital. Mac felt at once home and alien, a feeling that China often produced in him.

"Nice of you to give up your entire ICU," Mac said. "I don't see any patient with a craniotomy scar here."

"We didn't volunteer to give it up," Wang said. "The hospital is limiting neurosurgical cases that might need ICU beds. That's what the emergency meetings have been about."

Chow added. "Patients with this new disease get sick fast and need ICU care. Elderly people develop an intractable pneumonia in three days and drown in their own secretions."

Mac looked at Wang. "Sounds like a major problem. What do you think, Jin?"

"The numbers are certainly increasing."

"Soon we'll have to stop all surgery to make beds for these patients," Chow said. "Last Tuesday we had two with this severe pneumonia, this weekend four, today sixteen."

Mac did the math. Exponential increases.

Chow pulled them over to one bed. "Let me show you an example. This patient is forty-three years old. He came to us from prison yesterday. He was healthy two days ago but had extensive contact with pangolins. Last night he couldn't breathe. His chest X-ray shows extensive pneumonia. Today he needs one hundred percent oxygen and ten centimeters of PEEP to keep his pO2 at seventy."

"Pangolins?" Mac asked. He looked at Wang, then examined the patient's face more closely. "Jin, isn't that the man we saw in the live animal market yesterday?"

Wang scanned the man's face, then looked at the chart. "Yes, the same person. He comes from the countryside west of here. I'm afraid he will never make it back home."

Chow moved them on to the next bed. "This woman is only thirty, but she has diabetes. Came in with a forty-one-degree fever and chest pain. Even with ice cooling, maximum aspirin and fluids, her temperature is still forty."

"That's 104 degrees Fahrenheit," Wang said.

"I know," Mac replied.

"Her blood sugar is uncontrolled, and we can't keep her blood oxygen at a satisfactory level," Chow said. "She will probably die tonight."

"What do the sputum smears and cultures show in these patients?" Mac asked.

"Lots of white cells, but no bacterial growth on culture," Dr. Chow said. "Typical viral pneumonia. We convinced the virology lab down the street to do PCR. The early results suggest a coronavirus, but a new strain—"

She looked toward the door and grimaced. Mac saw the hospital director bearing down on them with narrowed eyes and clenched jaw. The man beckoned for Chow to step away and began shouting at her. Wang looked embarrassed and moved Mac out of the room.

"What's going on?" Mac asked.

"They're having a discussion."

Mac could still hear the angry voices, one escalating higher and louder than the other.

"That's more than a discussion, Wang. It's a blowup."

Wang dropped his shoulders and the corners of his mouth. "Dr. Chow has been complaining for two weeks about this so-called outbreak, advocating for better protective measures for our doctors and nurses."

"You mean gowns, masks, gloves?"

"Exactly. The hospital does not have a budget for them, so the administrators do not want to hear her complaints.

I think she hoped if she could persuade you, the officials would listen to you because you come from Boston."

"We still don't know whether this is going to be a significant outbreak," Wang said as they changed back to street clothes. "For the rest of the afternoon, I will show you our regular wards, the radiology department, and the outpatient clinic. Then you must talk with the residents and give your second lecture. Tonight, we will have a small dinner with our trainees."

As he toured the facility, Mac was reminded of veteran's hospitals he had visited in the United States. Built in the 1950's, the hospital persisted with linoleum floors, open wards, and iron beds. He felt a sense of relief when he stopped touring and could talk with the neurosurgical trainees.

He enjoyed discussions with residents more than any other of his visiting professor duties. At these informal meetings, he could get a sense of what concerned the new generation.

One of the senior neurosurgical residents stood out in the discussion. Named Meixiu Feng (or Feng Meixiu if he used the Chinese order of names, surname first), she was a mother of two children. She began neurosurgical training after her youngest child entered grade school.

Feng appeared to be as committed to her husband and children as to her career. She spoke excellent English and seemed aware of all the latest developments in neurosurgical management and technique. Mac left the session elated and encouraged about the next generation of doctors in China.

He must have carried that elation to his lecture, which dealt with problems of global neurosurgery, because the audience gave him a standing ovation at the end. Afterward he again engaged in a lively question and answer session. For the rest of the hospital visit, Mac continued in the glow of these encounters. This was what medical education should be—a free exchange of experience despite nationality and language.

Mac and Wang went straight from the hospital to dinner at a small restaurant in the neighborhood. A half-dozen trainees joined them. No dignitaries, no speeches, just a continuation of the informal discussions of the afternoon.

He was delighted to see Feng among the attendees. Over dinner they discussed the possibility of her coming to Boston for a postgraduate year.

Before he escorted Mac to the limousine, Wang told him that they had made one change in the schedule. They would visit the Wuhan virology institute the next morning. That scientific group, the most advanced in Wuhan, wanted to present some data on the new virus as they got it ready for publication.

CHAPTER FOUR

THE VIROLOGY LABORATORY

THURSDAY, JANUARY 2, 2020
WUHAN, CHINA

The Wuhan Institute of Virology looked like a building modelled on the National Institutes of Health in the USA. Two high-rise glass and concrete towers were separated by lower connector between them. The entire complex stood apart from the surrounding neighborhood on a manicured lawn

Standing beside Wang at the entrance was a thin man with grey hair. His eyes darted from side to side, as if he were anticipating a disturbance.

"This is Dr. Li, director-general of the Institute," Wang said.

Mac shook the director's offered hand.

"It is a propitious time to have you visit, Professor," Li said in perfect English. "We have some data for publication and are preparing for a review from your National Institutes of Health. We would be grateful for your input on our presentations."

"Great," Mac said, "but my expertise is brain tumors, not viruses."

"Science is science. I reviewed several of your publications on the molecular pathogenesis of glioblastomas and was quite impressed."

"I have to warn you that I will plan to be deliberately aggressive," Mac said. "It's better for you to face a hostile reviewer in the practice presentations than in the real site visit."

"That is fine with us," Li said. "Be as aggressive as you wish."

Wang smiled. "It looks like you two will get along fine. I have urgent administrative meetings all day about this new virus. Mac, can I leave you here and maybe join you for a quiet dinner at six?"

"Sounds great," Mac said. He turned back to the laboratory director. "A preliminary question before I spend the morning with you. The talk of SARS and this new illness yesterday concerned me. I'm used to pollution in the air in China, but I assume the air inside the building is filtered? I don't want to be inhaling viruses."

The director looked at Mac with raised eyebrows. "We are a Biosafety level 4 facility, the first and best in all of China. Our air is ultra-filtered. It is cleaner than any other air in Wuhan."

In the auditorium, twenty Chinese staff sat scattered, half filling the room.

Li began. "One of our major goals has been to understand the agent responsible for Severe Acute Respiratory

Syndrome, or SARS, that devastated us in 2003. Many people died in China then, but fortunately the outbreak could be contained and did not spread to the rest of the world. Today we are working on the novel virus we have just identified. Our data demonstrate that this is a cousin of SARS."

Mac raised his hand. "Where do you get support for this research?"

"We work under the direct authority of the Chinese Academy of Sciences and receive funding from the National Institutes of Health in America, the European Union, and the Chinese government."

"How does the NIH maintain quality control if you are 7500 miles away?" Mac asked.

Li looked annoyed, then seemed to remember that Mac had warned him he would be a hypercritical reviewer. "We prepare monthly quality assurance reports and have video cameras everywhere around our laboratories. Our procedures can be monitored any time."

Mac sat back in his chair, and Li called for the first scientist to present the lecture, "Introduction to Coronaviruses."

Mac's hand shot up before the lecturer could say a word. "Why are they called coronaviruses?"

The lecturer flicked on a slide showing dozens of small spheres with projections from them making a kind of halo. "This is an electron microscopic picture of coronaviruses. As you can see, their spikes make a crown—corona—around them."

"What are the spikes for?" Mac asked.

"They anchor the virus onto our lung cells."

"Same as SARS?"

"Yes, but this novel virus has a much higher affinity for the membrane than the SARS virus."

"If it's like SARS, why do you call it a novel virus?"

"Because it's new to humans as a race," the lecturer continued. "No one has natural immunity to it, and there is no so-called herd immunity."

"After the virus hooks onto the cell membrane, what does it do?" Mac continued.

The lecturer showed a diagram with the virus attached to the cell and injecting white strands. "It rips a hole in the cell membrane, injects its RNA, and hijacks the cell's manufacturing system to assemble more viruses. As you know, RNA is the template cells use to make protein. The newly-made viruses accumulate until they burst the cell and infect its neighbors."

"I just have one more question." Mac said. "How do you protect yourselves in these risky experiments?"

"We adhere strictly to the BSL-4 protocols."

Li thanked the speaker. "Shall we hear from Dr. Shi and his team now?"

A white-haired man hobbled to the podium and began. "Since 2003, we have been extracting coronaviruses from the excretions of bats in a cave in Yunnan, a thousand miles from here. We have shown bats in those caves are the source of the SARS virus."

"How did you get the specimens?" Mac asked.

"Our scientists explored the caves."

"And handled bat guano and urine and saliva?"

"Yes, but with the necessary precautions."

Mac remembered a Facebook picture of one of these investigators with bat urine dripping onto his bare scalp.

Dr Shi continued, "We determined that the horseshoe bats in that cave carried the coronavirus that produces SARS. We described the sequence in a paper in Nature. We later showed that it got to humans through civets, that is, that the virus learned to live in civets, then in humans. And we expressed concern that there was a village only a kilometer away from the bat caves, making transmission to those specific humans quite feasible."

He wiped his brow, looked at Mac, who said nothing, and continued. "Hospitals in Wuhan have recently asked us to analyze specimens from patients with this new viral pneumonia. The virus causing that pneumonia is similar to the SARS virus. It uses pangolins rather than civets as an intermediate to get to humans, but we believe it comes from bats in the same caves as the SARS coronavirus."

Mac sat through the rest of the lectures without interrupting, considering the fragile human bio-environment that surrounds all inhabitants of earth. Viruses, prions, bacteria, parasites, insects, animals, and humans live in an uneasy equilibrium. It does not take much to disturb the equilibrium and produce an ecological and biological disaster.

He hated bats. The idea of harvesting their secretions and the fact that a bat virus could infect humans made him nauseated.

He barely paid attention to the tour of the facility, murmuring approbation at the sparkling clean highly protected procedure rooms when prompted.

Invited to join for late lunch, he demurred. "My jet lag is worse than I anticipated. I will return to my hotel. I congratulate you on this excellent work."

"Of course," Li said. Mac thought he looked relieved that he would not have to face more intrusive questions. "I will arrange for the limousine to take you back now."

As he headed out of the building, Mac was stopped by a junior scientist who appeared anxious. "Thank you for your questions about how safe this facility is," he said in English that Mac could barely understand.

"Why? Are you worried?" Mac asked.

The man nodded his head, looking around. "I don't think the NIH guidelines are always followed."

"Have you told anyone?"

"My boss."

"And?"

"He told me not to bother about it, that we were doing the best we could."

"Is he still here? I'd like to talk with him."

"No. He died a week ago."

"Died?"

"Yes. We don't know what killed him."

"Could it have been the virus?"

"Don't know. Just know he died."

"Why are you telling me this?"

"I don't know who else to tell. If I say anything more to people here, I will be fired." He looked around to be sure no one stood nearby. "I don't believe you can do anything either. When you asked your questions, I started to worry about this again."

It took Mac two hours in the hired car to get back to the hotel. His body ached and he started to cough on the way.

Not feeling great, he texted Wang. *Can we postpone dinner?*

No problem, Wang texted back. *Urgent hospital meetings all day. Call if I can help.*

Mac again calculated the time difference between Wuhan and Boston—six p.m. here, so six a.m. there. He called up Lauren's smiling face on his phone a minute later.

"You OK?" she asked.

"Yes, just checking in."

"I forgot to ask you. Did you get to the live market?"

"Just got a glimpse of it. The government closed it down yesterday. Some strange new virus related to it. How are Maggie and Peter?"

"Acting up a little. We all miss you."

"Anything you want me to do or get while I'm here?"

"No. Return soon and safe."

"Love to everyone, especially you."

"Thank you, Cheri, and right back at you."

He decided there was no reason to be on his feet and collapsed into bed.

CHAPTER FIVE

SYMPTOMS

FRIDAY, JANUARY 3, 2020
WUHAN, CHINA

Mac woke up at three a.m. with a hacking cough. He drank half a bottle of water and took an aspirin from his shaving kit. He clicked on American TV, thinking about the paradox of watching an afternoon soap at three in the morning. His hacking did not abate, and his headache and chest pain worsened.

Something in the air at the Virology Institute, he thought as he propped himself on three pillows and drifted in and out of sleep.

He was glad to see six a.m. He took a hot shower, shaved, dressed, and coughed all the way to the hospital. A package of mints from the vending machine in the lobby did not help.

This morning he was scheduled to give his third and final lecture, and then operate with Wang at eleven a.m.

He made it through the lecture, thanks to slides that explained themselves. He would punch the next frame button and begin to speak, contort with a coughing fit, and signal to Wang to continue. Since the lecture was on brain tumor management, Wang knew most of the details. Mac, although he understood no Mandarin, had confidence that Wang would say the right thing. By the end of the lecture, Wang was delivering the lecture as the main speaker, with only brief prompts from Mac.

The talk was well-received, but Mac did not allow questions. "I'm not sure whether I will be safe in the operating room if I help you out today, either," he said to Wang. "I'd hate to be coughing all over someone's brain."

"We cancelled the case," Wang replied. "The hospital is discouraging elective surgery. Not only that, but our main scrub nurse, the only one I trust, got the sick yesterday and I don't want to operate without her."

"I may have a touch of the flu as well. If I take it easy for the rest of the day, I'm sure I'll be fine."

"Come to my office," Wang said. "I'll check your temperature."

"Thirty-seven degrees," he announced after he removed the thermometer. "Maybe a fever, maybe not. Here, take this medicine for your cough and go to the hotel. I'll call about six. We can have quiet dinner together."

By the time he got to the hotel, Mac was glad he had cancelled everything. He was alternatively shaking with cold and sweating, and his cough continued despite the medication. His body ached and he felt as tired as if he had run a marathon

He added extra blankets to his bed and found himself an hour later throwing them onto the floor as he sweated and burned. His chest pain increased, making each cough an agony. He gulped down some strong pain medicine he had brought with him in case of severe pain. It helped for a half hour. Then the agony returned.

Worst, however, were the hallucinations. His dead father hovered over the bed, opening his mouth to speak. Mac cowered under a pillow, tossing and turning to sleep.

By six p.m. he knew he needed medical help. He called for the house doctor and learned it would be three hours before the physician could be there. While he waited, he called Lauren to tell her he felt sick.

Lauren appeared to be shocked at his appearance on the WeChat screen.

"Mac, what happened?" she asked, raising her hand to her mouth.

"I don't feel very well," he said. "Maybe a cold I picked up on the plane. Or maybe I should have gotten that flu shot before I left."

"Do you have a fever? Have you seen a doctor?"

"I'm waiting now. I don't want to bother Dr. Wang. Too embarrassing."

"Will you be able to come home when you planned to?"

"I'm not sure. I'll let you know if I have to change the flights. I wouldn't be a great person to be around right now anyway. Can I see Maggie and Peter?"

"Sure. They need to get up for school in half an hour. It's still dark here. Give me a minute and I'll get them."

Mac stared at the screen and coughed as she roused the children.

"Daddy, it's too early," Maggie said. "I'm still waking up.'"

"That's OK, sweetheart. I just wanted to say good morning."

"Good morning." She waved. "Now can I go back to bed?"

"Sure, sweetie. Will you put your brother on?"

"Hi Dad. How's China?" Peter seemed awake and ready for the day. "Is it cold there? It's snowing here."

"No snow. It's more like March."

"Why are you coughing so much? Are you sick?"

"I think I picked up a cold."

"Well, I hope you feel better. Got to get ready for school. Bye."

Lauren returned. "It's great to see you even if you look—"

"Terrible? I'm glad you can't see how I feel."

"I love you, Mac. I can't wait for you to be home."

"Me too."

He clicked off the phone and waited with painful chest and shaking body until the doctor came.

The hotel physician was about fifty, with a British accent and very polished manner. He was careful to point out that, although a native-born Chinese, he had trained in Cambridge, England. After he examined Mac, he made the diagnosis of the flu. He provided antibiotics and added a traditional Chinese powder to make tea. He said the concoction would help stop the cough and kill the virus.

"Could I have something to sleep?" Mac asked. "If I could just get a good night's rest, I might feel a lot better."

The physician rummaged in his bag and took out a handful of pills. "Take one of these before you go to bed. It should let you drift off. I'll call in the morning to see how you are doing."

"Thank you. How do I pay you?"

"The hotel will put it on the bill."

Mac's coughing seemed to worsen the moment the doctor left the room. He took the cough syrup and another pain pill with no relief. He drank water, sucked lozenges, and tried to get to sleep.

Overnight, his cough did not abate. His chest felt as if it were on fire with every intake of air. He could never get a full breath. He also had a severe headache and thought he might be seeing something moving on the walls. He sat up all night.

The next morning Mac felt he might die. What was worse, his pain and shortness of breath led him to think that might be fine. He sucked on a lozenge to lubricate his throat, then stopped with fear gripping him even more strongly.

He could not taste the lozenge. No medicinal flavor, no sweetness, nothing at all. Might as well be plastic. He ripped a chocolate bar from the mini bar and put half of it in his mouth to see if he could taste it. It tasted like dry powder, though he could feel it melting in his mouth.

No common cold or flu or upper respiratory infection he had ever heard of produced loss of taste. As a neurosurgeon, he knew that what causes such loss had to be an invasion of the olfactory nerves that lay just above the nose. They led right to the brain.

Whatever was attacking him, it was going after his brain as well as his lungs.

His heart raced even faster, making his shortness of breath worse. He texted Wang, who arrived within half an hour.

Wang took one look at Mac and said, "We need to get you to the hospital. How could you get so sick in twenty-four hours?"

CHAPTER SIX

DETERIORATION

JANUARY 4-9, 2020
WUHAN, CHINA

"You're taking me to Zhongnan Hospital? Is there no private hospital in Wuhan?" Mac looked back toward the hotel as he staggered toward the car, considering a rebellious return to his room.

Wang eased him into the back seat. Mac lay down on it without complaining further. Was he slated to die in a public hospital in a foreign city?

"This country has only one citizen category, professor. We are all equal. No segregation by nationality or wealth."

"How about party officials? They go to this hospital?"

Wang nodded. "Yes. We'll take you to the VIP floor. Don't worry."

Everything in the admissions process was a blur. Faces flashed by. Questions asked in Mandarin got answered by Wang. Mac was too busy coughing, worsening the headache, and exacerbating the excruciating pain in his chest.

After helping Mac onto a stretcher, Wang injected

something into the intravenous line freshly placed in Mac's left hand. "Morphine," he said.

Mac's pain lessened and a feeling of warmth enveloped him. This must be why narcotics are so addicting, he thought as he drifted to sleep.

When he awoke, he found himself on a cot with a thin mattress and thinner bed cover. The air hung heavy with sweat and disinfectant. Alarms and monitors created a constant anxious undertone.

He checked his body. Oxygen prongs in his nose, cardiac monitor leads on his chest, and an IV in the left arm. A hospital johnny and his boxer shorts under it.

He lifted his head and surveyed his surroundings. Dozens of cots filled with coughing men lay around him in a large room with very narrow passageways between them. The cough was dry and non-productive, as annoying to hear as to have. The nurses and orderlies could hardly maneuver around the beds and wore no masks or other protection.

This could not be a VIP floor, Mac thought. He pressed a red button at his bedside. A nurse arrived within a minute. She was young and friendly, and asked him in English what he wanted, speaking through a cloth mask.

"Is this the VIP floor?" he asked.

"No rooms left in any floor. We are putting beds down in the clinic," she said. "You're on this floor because I am here, and I speak English. I spent time in Los Angeles."

She arranged his nasal prongs, injected something in the IV that again made him feel better, and turned away.

Over the next hour he spent his time coughing and trying

to find a comfortable position. He was delighted to see Jin Wang, who now wore a mask.

"What happened to me, Jin? I feel absolutely terrible."

"You have an infection from the new coronavirus. You, probably picked it up during our adventures the first day here."

"But we didn't go into the live animal market."

"Many people infected had nothing to do with the market. The authorities have shut it down anyway, just to be sure. Although we are still collecting data, it looks as if people without symptoms can spread the disease. You probably got it during one of our many excursions."

"Are you OK? You must have gotten a dose as well."

"To be truthful, I am not feeling very well, but I think it's just from the administrative meetings that are taking up all my time now. Anyway," Wang continued as he scanned Mac's chart, "Your oxygen level is still falling. We must switch to high-flow oxygen."

Mac didn't care what they did as long as it allowed easier breathing.

But the new oxygen level didn't help. Wang placed longer plastic prongs in his nostrils and a tight-fitting mask over his face. Mac now felt suffocated both by the mask and his inability to get air into the lungs. Breathing became a full-time effort.

"That's worse," he said to Wang. "Do I need a chest X-ray?"

"Not necessary. We know it will show a pneumonia whiting out both lungs."

"Could someone call my wife please?" Mac's thinking

was becoming erratic. He could not put a coherent train of thought together.

"I will try. Later," Wang replied.

If the first part of the day was gray, the rest faded to black. Mac felt sweat drip from his body. He fought for every breath, wrapping the thin bedcover around him when he was chill, throwing it off half an hour later when he was burning. His chest, head, and entire body ached. He felt as if a rhinoceros were on his chest, digging its tusks under his ribs. He felt more exhausted than ever in his life.

After a particularly violent bout of coughing followed by gulping for air and not getting any, he waved frantically to the nurse. He could not hear his voice and pointed to his throat.

The nurse's face looked down at him. Her shocked expression made him even more anxious. He heard the alarms, the sound of feet running toward him, then nothing.

He opened his eyes to chaos. Men and women rushed in and out of his visual field. Sighing of the ventilators sounded as if a thousand Darth Vaders had invaded the room. He could smell nothing.

He tried to take a deep breath and sit up but realized he could not control his own breathing. He tried to speak but nothing came. He was restrained to the bed by a sheet, but his hands were free. He felt for his mouth and realized he had a large tube in his left nostril.

I've been intubated. But where am I?

He felt around the mattress to find the call button pinned to the sheets. He pressed it, not sure what to expect. Perhaps an entire code blue team would materialize, thinking he was signaling a cardiac arrest.

Instead Dr. Feng, the senior resident with whom he had conversed so congenially, appeared at the edge of his vision. She leaned over and answered his unspoken question.

"Professor, you are in the ICU. You just had a respiratory arrest. Please do not breathe against the ventilator. We are giving you positive pressure. If you keep trying to breathe over the respirator, we will have to put you in coma."

He felt like throttling her. Why could he not take the big breath he needed? He needed to get enough oxygen into his lungs. And the tube made his nose uncomfortable.

He tried adding a quick breath in between ventilator sighs, but the alarm rang. He coughed, and the alarm rang. He moved in bed to get comfortable, and the alarm rang.

Feng appeared again. "You can't keep doing this, professor. You will increase your intracranial pressure and hurt your lungs. We're going to sedate you now."

He heard voices speaking Chinese directly beside him. He squinted to focus. A cluster of people with protective equipment. He recognized Feng's voice. "We will stop your ventilator now and let you breathe as you wish," she said. "No more sedation. If you are stable for four hours, we will take out your tube. Please cooperate."

A moment later he could take a breath. Sort of. It was like trying to get all his oxygen through a straw. He still could not avoid the pain in his chest when he took a breath in. He clenched his teeth and said nothing.

He must have dozed again, because he woke to a strange voice with a heavy accent shouting in his ear. "Professor, we are going to take out your tube. You may cough. Now take a big breath."

He felt a searing pain in the middle of his chest, coughed violently with sputum and blood, and lay back exhausted.

An oxygen mask clamped over his face.

"How long was I out?" he asked.

"Four days."

He thought he recognized Feng's voice.

"Meixiu, is that you?"

"Yes, professor."

"Did you say four days?" He frowned. Was it possible to forget four complete days?

"Yes. It's January ninth."

"What happened to me?"

"You developed bad lung problems. We thought we might lose you two or three times. Your lungs filled up with fluid. After a couple of days, you got better."

"I need to speak with my wife Lauren. She'll be horribly worried."

"I have talked to her every day. To Peter and Maggie too. They are so nice. You are right that they are worried. With luck, we can clean you up and get you to the real VIP ward tomorrow. They have WiFi there, so you could probably do a video chat."

"Could I make an audio call right now?"

"I have to retrieve your phone from security. Meanwhile, why don't you use mine?" Feng handed Mac her own phone, open and already ringing 'MacGregor family'.

"Meixiu?" Lauren's voice sounded anxious and tired "You're calling early. Is something wrong? Is Mac OK?"

Mac checked the time. Five p.m. here, five a.m. in Boston.

"Yes. OK," he answered.

Silence.

He thought perhaps the line had disconnected, but the seconds kept mounting on the call timer.

Then, very softly. "Mac? Is that you? Really you? Are you all right?"

Mac heard sobs from the phone. He tried to speak and could not. His throat and the virus and fatigue and despair seized him. Tears filled his eyes. He tried to speak several times, then handed the phone to Feng and lowered his head.

"Hi, Mrs. MacGregor. This is Meixiu. Yes, that was Professor MacGregor. Yes, he's all right. We just extubated him. No, I just think he was overwhelmed. I will."

She handed the phone back to Mac. Lauren's voice, now steady, came through as if she had been in the next bed. "Just listen, my love. I know it's hard to talk. We have missed you like crazy and been so afraid. Meixiu has been a godsend. We are all fine except for worrying about you. Please call me when you can. I love you."

"You have a wonderful wife, Professor," Feng said as she retrieved the phone.

Mac nodded. He was too exhausted to speak.

"And I think we will be able to get you out of the ICU now. To be honest, we need your bed for other patients."

CHAPTER SEVEN

RECOVERY

JANUARY 9-14, 2020
WUHAN, CHINA

The ward Mac transferred to seemed more orderly than his previous one. When Feng visited, she told him it was occupied by patients getting over their infection.

It boasted WiFi reception, and Mac could call Lauren and the children. It was not the same as a joyous reunion in person, but a kind of peace settled on him as he saw the two children and Lauren, healthy and energetic. The kids talked about their schoolwork and how scared they had been when they heard he was sick.

He ignored the stares of the other men in the room, none of whom displayed a cell phone.

"Are you hearing anything about this novel virus from Wuhan?" Mac asked Lauren after the children had finished their conversations.

"NPR had a piece on the fact that south China has an uptick in patients with a new illness. No sign of any big problems outside China. It seems remote to us."

"It's devastating here," Mac said.

He noticed a man in a drab brown suit standing at the foot of the bed. He was Asian, like everyone else around Mac, but was beefier. He seemed to be listening intently to the conversation.

"Excuse me," Mac said, expecting the man to move.

He did, but toward Mac. "I'm sorry. We do not allow overseas phone calls from the hospital," he said in good English as he swiped the phone from Mac and retreated. "You will get your phone back when you are discharged."

"Hey!" Mac called as the man disappeared. Mac tried to step out of bed, but his legs collapsed as he put weight on them. He pulled the emergency alarm and when the nurse covering the ward answered, he explained what had happened.

She shrugged her shoulders and left.

Mac cursed her lack of concern.

A few minutes later the English-speaking nurse reappeared.

"My colleague sends apologies," she said. "She does not understand English. What's the problem?"

He explained what happened.

"I'm sorry," she said. "It is a new policy. Staff cannot make calls from the wards either. Maybe what they say will frighten people outside. The administration is worried about how serious this infection seems to be."

"This is outrageous. How do I reach Dr. Wang, the chairman of neurosurgery? I'll tell him about this."

"You cannot reach him. He is a patient in the ICU upstairs."

Mac felt his stomach twist. "He's upstairs? Does he have

the same pneumonia?" The problem with the telephone suddenly seemed trivial.

"Yes. He came into the hospital just two days after you."

"I am sorry. How is he doing?"

"Not too well. He seems to be getting worse."

Mac had no idea whether China had the equivalent of HIPAA. In the United States, asking randomly about a patient not under your care would get you reprimanded or fired. He would take his questions up with Dr. Feng.

"Thank you. I'm sorry to bother you."

He lay considering the ironic twist that made Wang and him coronavirus patients together. Were the excursions they took so enthusiastically the day he arrived in Wuhan the source of the infection? If the virus is spread from human to human, that seemed the obvious source.

He asked Feng when she appeared later in the day. "I didn't know Wang was in the hospital. Is he going to make it?"

"I did not have an opportunity to tell you. He is still quite sick and intubated."

"If he wakes up, please tell him I am praying for him."

"I will. The nurse said you had a problem with your phone."

"They took it away. Can I borrow yours again?"

"I'm sorry. No. The administration has prohibited any calls from patients. I have been calling your family from my home and will continue to do that. If they see me with a phone on this ward, it will be confiscated. I'm even worried that they will track my home calls to the US and consider me a foreign agent."

"What do you suggest I do?"

"Get strong fast and go back to the hotel. Call from there."

Mac had never before experienced the sensation that his mind was disconnected from his muscles. As he started his rehabilitation, he could hardly walk despite knowing what his legs had to do. In trying something as simple as putting one foot in front of another, he found his mental command far ahead of his legs. His sense of balance was also off. He felt immensely fatigued after a fifteen-minute session.

His physiotherapy took place in the corridors of the hospital, supervised by nurses' aides who seemed young enough to be high school students. In doing his exercises he passed dozens of masked patients trying to regain their strength and balance. The effect was like a caricature of rush hour in the subway. Crowds pushed one way, then the other, in a moebius strip of activity without a destination.

He no longer thought it stifling to have a multitude doing just what he was doing. Just the opposite. He enjoyed the silent camaraderie of other patients pushing themselves to get atrophied legs and arms to work.

And to heal their inflamed brains. Mac had felt a fog over his mental processes for a week. Only now did he realize that it too was part of the viral infection. His taste had slowly come back to normal, but his thinking still had a kind of fantastic quality about it. Things around him sometimes changed colors or shape and swirled. The phenomenon always went away if he waited a few seconds or stopped what he was doing.

His continuous coughing and chest pain did not help, because every cough made his head hurt. The hacking did improve each day.

As his thinking got clearer, he missed more and more the

opportunity to talk with his family. Improving so he could connect with video was a strong incentive to get out of the hospital.

After four days he began to feel strong enough to be independent. He got to enjoy the meal of rice and gravy that was the hospital staple. He could get himself to the bathroom and back. He could take a deep breath without wincing in agony.

Feng came to his bedside that afternoon. "You can go back to the hotel tomorrow."

"Am I ready? How do I keep in touch?" Having looked forward to this moment for days, Mac realized how completely he now depended on this woman.

"You can call me whenever you want."

"When do you think I could fly home?"

"Not for a week at least. Here is your phone. Don't use it in the hospital tonight. Tomorrow I will not be here. So good luck."

They shook hands, and Mac watched with sadness as she walked away. He was glad to leave the hospital, but felt he was also leaving the cocoon of safety that Feng helped spin.

On January fourteenth, ten days after he had entered as a patient, Mac left Zhongnan Hospital.

The hotel room, which had been held for him, seemed sterile, large, and unfriendly. He had learned to enjoy tight quarters and anonymous fellow travelers.

He sat on his bed realized how much his harrowing experience had changed him. He would never again disdain the work done in city or state hospitals to treat everyone who came through their doors. He would remember forever the sense of friendliness and mutual respect that infused both the health care workers and their patients.

And above all, he realized how much humans inhabit one world together. Lauren's comment that it all seemed so far away and irrelevant to them was just plain wrong. Members of the species *Homo sapiens* exist because they can band together and help one another.

Somewhere deep in his brain he believed this virus was going to change the world forever.

It was eleven p.m. Boston time. He decided he would call Lauren despite the late hour. Her face brightened immediately on seeing him. Heavy-lidded eyes told him she had been wakened out of sleep.

She commented that the room looked like a hotel, not a hospital ward. "Meixiu told me you'd be leaving today. Are you out?"

"Yes, and I don't feel too bad considering I almost died."

"Please don't say that, Mac. You have no idea how horrible it is to be 7500 miles away from someone you love when it looks as if he's going to die."

"The same from the other end."

"When can you come home?"

"I don't know, but I'm working on it as hard as I can. As soon as I can walk and think straight, I'll let you know."

CHAPTER EIGHT

GIVING BACK

JANUARY 14-17, 2020
WUHAN, CHINA

Mac spent the first two hotel days working to get his strength back. He had the exercise facility to himself, went from rowing machine to elliptical and back. He felt his strength returning. More important for him, his thinking, which had been confused and erratic, returned towards normal.

The phone calls with Feng disturbed him. She said their hospital was overwhelmed, as was every other in Wuhan. They asked for help from other cities, but it would take a few days to arrive.

"Would I be useful?" he asked.

"You mean, as a doctor?"

"Yes. Since I got sick, I'm presumably immune to the virus."

"Let me call you back."

In ten minutes, she returned the call. "The administrator says that would be all right. They already gave you temporary licensing to see patients with Dr. Wang before you got here."

"How is Dr. Wang doing?"

"Very slow. You could see him if you wish. Could you help for three hours tomorrow morning?"

The next morning Mac sat at the desk of the same intensive care unit he had occupied as a patient the week before. Feng stayed close, translating his orders and sometimes adding in her opinion about what the appropriate steps would be to solve a problem, as she knew more about the culture than he.

Mac paid particular attention to the man in bed eight. It was Dr. Jin Wang, his Chinese host. Wang was still intubated and sedated. Several times, Mac went over and talked to him. He squeezed Wang's hand as he spoke words of encouragement and noted that he sometimes squeezed back.

By noon, Mac was exhausted. At home, he easily worked fourteen hours at a time. Here, three had wiped him out. He asked to go back to the hotel, which Feng was happy to arrange. As he was leaving, Mac asked her about Dr. Chow, the doctor who had advocated for better personal protective equipment.

"She should be considered a hero, but she has disappeared."

"What do you mean disappeared?"

"No one can find her. I've talked to her brother. She's not sick as far as they know, and she's not with her family."

Feng looked around as if to check for people who might overhear. "Sometimes these things happen in China. The country is changing but it's not free like America. She went to the press and made public statements which the officials did not like. That is sometimes enough to make a person disappear. No one knows what happens to him or her."

Back in the hotel, Mac went right to bed. Every cell in his body complained about overwork, the kind of fatigue that he used to get after a twelve-hour case. Still, he was happy to help. He slept, as he would say in the past, "like an intern."

He woke reasonably refreshed the next morning and arrived on the ward to find that Wang had deteriorated significantly. Feng stood at the side of his bed.

"What happened?" Mac asked.

"His oxygen saturation dropped to twenty despite everything we could do. That's not enough oxygen to keep the brain alive. He's lost all neurological activity."

Mac did a quick exam on his host. Wang had no breathing or movement, showed fixed and dilated pupils, had no response to touching his cornea with a tissue, and did not cough when his endotracheal tube was manipulated. Electroencephalogram leads protruded from his scalp.

"We're doing an EEG to confirm brain death," Feng said.

"His temperature's normal?" Mac asked.

"Yes."

"No sedating drugs?"

"Correct."

"Blood pressure in normal range?"

"Yes. As your questions suggest, we have made sure all confounding conditions have been eliminated."

"Does the hospital have a policy concerning ventilation for patients who have met criteria for brain deanth?"

"Yes, we stop the artificial breathing machine."

"Let's see the EEG."

He looked at the flatline curve on the screen displayed the brain wave machine. "Dr. Feng, I'm sorry to tell you that my friend, your chief, is dead."

"We'll remove the breathing tube and ventilator as soon as we have the official reading. Do you agree with that course of action?"

"Yes, of course," Mac said. "There's no point ventilating a dead person."

"I will talk with his relatives and make all the arrangements for his cremation," Feng said. "It is a terrible loss for all of us. We could never get his lungs to work."

In better circumstances, Mac would have spent considerable time cursing the death of a former postdoctoral fellow who had become a friend. His Wuhan host had succumbed to a virus he had hoped would be "not much trouble." Mac realized then how disastrous it was to deny the power of this virus.

The experience of seeing so many sick patients numbed Mac to the reality of this tragedy. He had no tears left to flow.

He moved on to the thirty other patients in the intensive care unit. Examining them one by one with Feng, he tried to prescribe treatment and assess who would be most likely to live. He could not rid his mind of the friend he had just lost and the cursed virus that had caused the death.

He felt emotionally dead, as if he were living a fearful nightmare he could not awaken from. As a physician, he recognized the shutting down of feeling that comes with overwhelming psychic trauma. The knowledge did not improve the hopelessness he felt.

On his break, he walked through the rest of the hospital. All wards and corridors were packed with people in different phases of treatment. The bottom two floors were designated for patients who had simply contracted the disease and did not need ventilatory support to breathe. About two hundred men and women lay coughing and writhing as he had, waiting to see what would happen next. Patients were added as they entered, with no regard for gender.

The surgical floors, including the ICUs, had been dedicated to patients who needed assisted ventilation. The recovery room, the operating rooms, and all the former ICUs had been made into intensive care units. Two operating rooms were held open for emergencies, but all elective surgery was canceled.

The top three floors of the hospital contained people who were recovering. They were kept in the hospital until they could get back on their feet. They would then be sent home or to a longer-term rehabilitation facility. They paced the halls as he had done, trying to get their strength back, waiting to get into bathrooms, signing up for showers, swapping stories of their lives before their coronavirus attacks.

Everywhere, patients and health care personnel wore masks. Often, they could only be distinguished from patients by the protective gowns they wore.

As he left the hospital, Mac saw busloads of nurses and physicians arriving from other cities to help. They were tested for fever by military police, then directed to the administrative offices where their beds had been set up. Large trucks delivered protective equipment including masks, gowns, hats, and shoe covers.

After three days, Mac felt he was no longer needed to help with patients. Hundreds of Chinese doctors had arrived from other parts of the country. He could not speak Mandarin and therefore could not communicate with doctors or patients. Dr. Feng had to attend to her own residency duties and should not be expected to stay with him as a translator.

He was not familiar with some of the equipment being used. His knowledge of ventilator settings was not as good as some of the doctors arriving, and he could not be taught as they could because he spoke only English.

He sat drained of all energy on his hotel bed and decided he might be more helpful in other ways. He made a long overdue phone call

CHAPTER NINE

WUHAN AND THE CDC

SATURDAY, JANUARY 18, 2020
WUHAN, CHINA

Mac's call went to Russ Baxter, a classmate Mac had kept up with occasionally since medical school. Baxter had recently been appointed Deputy Director of Atlanta's Centers for Disease Control and Prevention, the governmental agency charged with coordinating America's response to epidemics.

"Haven't heard from you for a while, Mac. Everything OK?" Russ asked.

"No. I'm calling from China. From Wuhan."

Mac could hear Baxter sit up and change tone.

"What the hell are you doing there?" Baxter asked.

"I came to be visiting professor for a week."

"Bad timing. What's it like there? We can't get accurate information."

"It's terrible. I caught the virus and have just been released from the hospital. I wouldn't wish COVID-19 on my worst enemy. When it gets to America, you're going to find a lot of deaths."

"We don't think it will cross the ocean," Russ said. "It'll stay in Asia the way SARS did. No cases reported here. What starts in China stays in China. We're not even sure it is transmitted from one person to another."

"Believe me, it is. I got it from the crowds around me, and it's spreading quickly in Wuhan. There are twelve million people in this city who interact with others all over the world. It won't stay here. It's going to spread everywhere, and America needs to be ready."

"I guess we'll have to cross that bridge when we come to it."

"Baxter, don't you hear what I'm saying? This virus will infect the whole United States. It's coming to Georgia and New York and Mississippi and everywhere in the United States. Have you ever known me to be an alarmist? Not much fazes me. But this is going to be one of the worst things you've ever had to deal with."

Baxter said nothing. Mac could imagine him twirling a pencil between his fingers, as he always did when he was deciding something. "Look, Mac," he finally said. "I'm in a bit of an awkward place here. The official position is that this virus is nothing. All we're supposed to do is observe whatever news comes from other countries."

"You'll be sorry for that policy."

"Let me finish. Observing means having good data. Would you be willing to be our man on the ground in Wuhan?"

"Probably not. I don't want to be an American spy."

"It would be more like being an official medical observer."

"I don't think so."

"Jesus Christ, Mac, you just called me to tell me there's a potential problem. Now you say you won't take the trouble to be part of the solution."

"From what I've seen of the present American administration, I'm not sure they're interested in the solution."

"The CDC would be. Let me see what my superiors say."

Mac called Dr. Feng while he was waiting for Baxter's return call. "Would you be willing to take some time off patient care to help with long-range planning for the city of Wuhan?"

"What do you mean?"

"I may be invited to be an official at the Wuhan response to the virus's spread. I need a translator, but more important, I would appreciate having a smart colleague to work with."

"My proper place is on the wards."

"It would be safer for your family to have you out of active duty for several hours a week."

"I'll discuss it with my husband. How are you? Are you recovering?"

"I'm incredibly weak, but my brain seems to be working again. I can put together two coherent thoughts. No more hallucinations, and I can taste again. My chest still hurts when I cough and my body feels like it's been twisted and crushed, but I see light at the end of the tunnel."

Baxter called a few minutes later. "Interesting response to my proposal, Mac. My immediate superior at the CDC was enthusiastic about the idea of deputizing you. When he checked it with his boss at the Department of Health and Human Services, he got a soft stonewall."

"How could you have a soft stone?"

"It wasn't a no or a yes. There seems to be a desire in official circles to hide our head in the sand and deny that there is a problem. Our superiors at the Department of Health and Human Services say they want no official involvement of DHHS with what China is doing. Any outbreak must be perceived as a Chinese problem, not one that will affect America. This policy appears to come right from the White House."

"Don't they realize the world is too small to think this is a Chinese problem only?" Mac said.

"I don't know what they realize or don't. We propose a compromise. Our division of emerging zoonotic diseases can appoint you as a civilian consultant to learn about the Wuhan experience and their response. As an observer, you would be independent of any official governmental institute. I'll make the authorization as general as possible, which should get you into Wuhan's decision-making circles. After that, it's up to you what you do with your seat at the table."

That satisfied Mac. The dispatch from the CDC was relayed quickly, and by four o'clock he received an invitation from the mayor of Wuhan to join the strategic planning council for coronavirus infection. The council met by teleconference on WeChat daily, the email said, with the next meeting at 10 a.m. the next day.

Mac quickly obtained permission for Feng to join as his

translator and made an agreement with the business center of the hotel to allow them to sit together during the meetings.

He then got tested both for the virus and for antibodies. His nasal swab showed that he had no active virus in his nose and his serum results demonstrated that he had high concentration of antibodies. That meant it was safe for Feng to sit with him for four hours each morning. She could cut her work on the wards by four hours a day, which made her happy. She had to sign a document to ensure complete secrecy about the meeting proceedings. He soon understood why that document was necessary.

CHAPTER TEN

COUNCIL

JANUARY 19-20, 2020
WUHAN, CHINA

As the videoconference started the next morning, Mac already knew three of the members of the special council. The mayor, now with open shirt collar and no suit jacket, enthusiastically welcomed him, pointing out they had already dined together. The hospital director similarly extended a warm welcome. He noted that Dr. MacGregor was in the unique position to see the epidemic from both sides, as patient and as doctor.

Dr. Li, head of the Wuhan Virology Laboratory, seemed less effusive in his welcome. Mac thought perhaps he was still smarting from the questions Mac had asked during his visit to the laboratory.

One of the people unknown to Mac interrupted. “I did not know we would have an American representative here. That was not part of the protocol.”

The mayor seemed prepared for this question. He shot back, “Comrade Chang, doesn’t the Central Committee get copied on all official documents from Beijing related to this matter? Professor MacGregor comes as a representative of the American CDC. I'm sure your associate from our own CDC can vouch for that institution."

A woman nodded and said something that Mac could not hear, but seemed to appease the first man.

Introductions continued. Mac was delighted to meet, figuratively speaking, the public health representative. She carried a PhD from the Chan School of Public Health at Harvard. She noted with a smile that her time rotating on the neurosurgery service at Harbor Hospital convinced her to stick to population health instead of neurology. The problem of dealing with disorders of the nervous system was too emotionally draining.

Mac pointed out with a frown that public health was also quite stressful right now and decided to name her Public Health Rep in his mind.

The other five team members seemed intelligent and eager. Mac thought of one of them as the 'Objector', the man who previously opposed Mac's presence. He represented the Central Committee in Beijing and seemed to speak English well. Mac understood why he might not want an American as an observer on the hottest spot in China.

The second was the representative of the Chinese Center for Disease Control, modelled on the American CDC. She seemed friendly and again had a good sense of English. She became 'Ms. CDC'.

The other three spoke Mandarin only: the financial manager for Wuhan, the chief of police, and the manager for trash and waste disposal in the city. Mac had no snappy names for them.

Feng did a remarkable job of simultaneous translation throughout the meeting. The mayor addressed Mac to begin. "Professor MacGregor, you should understand that our function as public officials is to guard the health and well-being of all our citizens. Every person is important, including old people and sick people. We must identify and control threats to everyone's health."

Mac wondered whether most American politicians could make this statement. Didn't most of them seek to please the majority as their primary goal, rather than do what was best for even their disadvantaged constituents?

The mayor continued, "The SARS epidemic taught those of us in government administration that transparency, expert advice, and decisive action were keys to protecting our people. This council is empowered to make whatever rules are necessary to limit the present outbreak."

The Objector asked, "Let us move onto real issues. Can someone seem perfectly well and still infect others with the virus?"

"Yes," Public Health Rep answered. "Our testing of asymptomatic patients shows that is possible."

"And what is the treatment for someone who is positive but has no symptoms?" Objector continued.

"Isolate them from their family for fourteen days," public health rep replied.

"So exactly who will need isolation, and for how long?" Ms. CDC asked.

"Apart from patients with clinical signs of infection, we

will also need to isolate citizens who test positive even if they have few or no symptoms, and contacts of patients who test positive. They will all need fourteen days of isolation."

Mac scribbled furiously to keep up. Feng, who translated effortlessly, helped make his notes accurate. He thought of the implications if this virus got to America. Staggering. Millions of tests needed, and the necessity to segregate asymptomatic people. How would that go down in Texas?

"Why do people die?' the chief of police asked.

Mac answered, "The virus attacks the lungs and makes them unable to get oxygen to the body because of the secretions and inflammation. ICU's, ventilators, and trained personnel are needed."

"How many ventilators, and how many personnel, do you think will be necessary?" the hospital administrator asked.

"For the entire city, at least twenty thousand ventilators and fifty thousand added health care workers," Public Health Rep said.

The discussion continued for several hours, mixing hard data and best guesses. By two p.m. everyone including Mac admitted to being ready to stop.

"I believe we have enough information for the day," the mayor said. He thanked them all and assigned a job to each member of the team including Mac. "Dr. MacGregor, can you think about how to find the large number of hospital beds we will need in the various categories we have discussed?"

Mac could hardly keep his eyes open as he flicked off the computer. Feng wished him a good day and left for the hospital.

Mac had planned to walk along the water outside the hotel but felt so fatigued from the meeting he returned straight to his room from the business center. He did his daily rehab exercises, ordered room service food, watched CCTV, the only channel available, and fell asleep.

The next morning, the public health rep began.

"I must now introduce you to R, the number of other citizens a person carrying the virus will infect. With an R of 3, one sick person will be responsible for infecting 56,000 people after ten cycles of contact. We have to bring R to zero or we will soon have two hundred thousand patients needing hospitalization."

"No way we can manage that," the administrator said.

"And we can't afford to build new hospitals," the financial manager said.

"But we can't let people just die," Ms. CDC said.

"Which brings us to the question I asked Dr. MacGregor to consider last night," the mayor said. "Dr. MacGregor, have you thought about how we might accommodate all the extra patients we anticipate?"

"I believe I have a solution," Mac said. "The military uses tents for mobile hospitals which can be set up quickly. We could set up tent hospitals for the time needed."

"Would they be used for every type of patient involved?" Objector asked.

"No. Consider three grades of care. Grade one would be an observation and isolation unit for patients on quarantine, grade two for recovering patients, and grade three—the traditional hospital—should be reserved only for symptomatic patients. Grades one and two could be tents or other facilities repurposed—for example, hotels or convention centers. The important idea is that traditional hospitals should not be used for asymptomatic or recovering cases."

"A brilliant idea," the Objector said.

After two hours of discussion, the committee presented its plan.

1. Wuhan would soon be locked down.
2. Traditional hospitals would be closed to all patients except COVID-19 or emergency patients.
3. New low acuity temporary hospitals would monitor recovering or asymptomatic patients. Those facilities would be run by nurses with medical supervision.

They asked Mac his thoughts about the feasibility of such a plan. He said that in the States, mobilizing to meet these requirements would be difficult. "But I noted what you did to make Expo 2010 happen in Shanghai. China's ability to act definitively and swiftly is a remarkable achievement."

He saw several smiles.

"If you think those goals are impossible, wait until you hear this one," Ms. CDC said. "The measures we just talked about would bring R down to one—that is, one person might infect one other."

She drew a big X through the R=1 graph. "We need to get R down to zero. For that, we have to isolate contacts as well as symptomatic or asymptomatic patients. Every person who might have the disease, had contact with someone with the disease, or tested positive must be isolated for fourteen days away from others."

"That can never work," Mac said, forgetting his manners.

"It's one thing to isolate sick people, but to take those without symptoms—"

"This is China, not the USA," the mayor of Wuhan said. "If we must follow these guidelines to eradicate the virus, we will."

"I've got to see this," Mac said. "I don't think you'll get past first base."

At the puzzled looks, Feng explained the application of baseball to this discussion. Smiles broke out one by one as the attendees seemed to understand.

The mayor gave each of the participants homework to do for the next day. The Objector sent a private chat request to Mac to stay on the conference link after everyone else left.

"I didn't think your presence would add anything," he said. "But your suggestion of tent hospitals was useful, and I have enjoyed your comments about our planning. I bring you a comment from our Central Committee that we are happy that an American doctor can be part of our group."

"I'm not really a public health doctor," Mac said, "but thank you."

"We are very committed to avoid the errors we made during the SARS outbreak. By trying to suppress information, we delayed world management."

"Your action is much improved with this present outbreak."

"We hope so. After SARS, eighty percent of the people involved in the governmental decision-making lost their jobs. We don't want that to happen this time."

CHAPTER ELEVEN

MITIGATION

JANUARY 21-22, 2020
WUHAN, CHINA

On Tuesday morning the group progressed from theory to implementation. Each member reported on the resources available or required.

Chinese military and manufacturing companies amassed 100,000 square meters of tent. Beds from hotels, military encampments and school dormitories arrived by the hundreds. Hospital supplies and personal protective equipment came from Shanghai, Beijing, Guanzho, and every other major city in China.

The army would be the enforcement arm, overseen by one of the members of the central government delegation.

The lockdown would begin at ten a.m. January twenty-third. Bus, train, ferry, taxi, and airplane service would be stopped. All schools and office buildings would be closed. Shops, restaurants, and other stores would be shuttered except for grocery stores and pharmacies. Social distancing would be enforced, and masks and gloves would be necessary in all public areas.

Testing would be carried out on as many citizens as possible. "Until asymptomatic carriers could be found and isolated, we cannot bring R below one," the public health official said.

Mac interpreted this to mean the disease could never be controlled. How could you identify carriers without symptoms? Test twelve million people? And if, for example, children were identified who had the virus but no symptoms, could you really isolate them from their family?

As he was mulling the implications of the committee's decisions, he realized that the January twenty-third deadline had a significant implication for him personally. It was two days away. No one knew how long the lockdown would be. If he didn't get out by ten a.m. on the twenty-third, he would be trapped in Wuhan for weeks, or possibly months.

He tried to book a flight from Wuhan leaving in the next forty-eight hours and found it impossible. The rumor of a lockdown had spread widely.

He called Feng, explaining his problem.

"Why would you want to use a plane to get to Shanghai?" she asked. "The fast train is more comfortable and gets you there in the same time. Hold on."

"The options even by train are limited," she said when she returned to the line. "I have booked you a business ticket on the high-speed train to Shanghai which leaves at 1:09 a.m. on the twenty-third. It's the only ticket left. I will come by your hotel at 9 p.m. to pick you up. I anticipate it will be very crowded around the station."

"Thank you so much. How much do I owe you?"

"One hundred forty American dollars. Pay me after you get home."

"What about flights from Shanghai to America?"

"Should be no problem, but book that flight now. There should be lots of options once you are out of Hubei province."

Hainan Airways had a direct flight from Shanghai to Boston. He booked a business class ticket, then called his hospital to report he would be there in four days.

He didn't expect the response he got.

"Don't bother to come in for a month," the chief medical officer said. "No one wants to mingle with a surgeon who has just been in Wuhan. And I understand you actually came down with this bat virus. We don't want any of China's troubles here."

"How did you know I got sick?"

"I talked to a doctor named Feng and to the hospital administrator there. They said at one point you almost died."

"I'm slowly getting better, but I'm not right yet. Who's taking care of my patients."

"Dr. Pedroza. I don't know why she does it."

"I would do the same for her. And I trust her completely."

"Good. That will make your time off easier. I don't want to see you for a month."

Mac shook his head. He had grown up in a time when the hospital took care of its staff. Those days were over.

"Thanks for your support," he said, hoping the sarcasm would be evident from his tone.

"Sure," the chief medical officer said and hung up.

He called Dr. Julia Pedroza, his trusted staff colleague. "Thanks so much for covering my patients."

"You're welcome. We were all so worried. How are you feeling?"

"Better. I just hope this never comes to Boston."

"Are you OK now?"

"I'm coming back this week, but I need to put myself on quarantine for a few days until the tests come back."

"Why? Can you get the virus twice?"

"Perhaps. No one is sure."

"Do you need a place to stay on quarantine?"

"Yes."

"My brother-in-law is in Colombia with the family. His Dartmouth Street condo is empty."

"Do you think he would let me use it? That would be perfect."

"I bet he would be delighted to have someone take care of it. I'll check with him, but you should count on staying there. We miss you. Will you give me a call when you get in?"

"Absolutely. And thank you again."

Mac talked with Lauren next, telling her that he planned to be home in three days but would have to spend the first few days in isolation. The exact number of days would depend on the availability of testing and how quickly he could get the results.

"Do you really think it's that big a deal, Mac? No one here seems to think the virus is a problem."

"They will think differently in a month. And I don't want you or the kids to become patients to show them how big a problem it can be."

The next day he signed onto the Wuhan council Zoom conference, said his thank yous and goodbyes to the other members, and decided to walk before packing.

The change in the city astounded him. When he arrived, frenetic activity had characterized this huge metropolis. Immense traffic jams, bustling crowds on the sidewalks, and street-side vendors were the norm.

Now he saw few people walking. Everyone wore masks. The grocery stores had long lines in front of them. When he looked through the doorway, he could see only empty shelves. Most other stores were shuttered with signs in the window saying simply "CLOSED" in English and/or Mandarin.

Dismayed, he returned to the hotel, packed his small suitcase, and slept until it was time to leave for the train station.

CHAPTER TWELVE

DEPARTURE

THURSDAY, JANUARY 23, 2020
WUHAN, CHINA

Although its clock read 12:05 a.m., the Wuhan train station crackled with activity. Shrill voices rose above the hum of car engines idling as their vehicles tried to get close enough to drop off passengers. A chill wind whistled through the open plaza, dispersing the smell of oil emitted by the idling engines. LED streetlamps half-illuminated the scene, throwing faces into flickering images that merged and lengthened in grotesque shadow play.

Mac thought they had allowed plenty of time to get to the train, but the streets around the station had become a six-block parking lot. When they took an hour to travel thirty meters, he looked at Feng, nodded, and they both hopped out of the taxi. Mac gave the driver an additional hundred yuan, then bounced his carry-on along the sidewalk to follow Feng's brisk pace.

A crush of people of all ages thronged the walkway that led into the station. Most of them wore cloth masks. A few had latex gloves as well. Soldiers equipped with QBZ-95 assault rifles monitored the crowd but did not interfere with the tight conjunction of one person with another.

It took several minutes to squeeze through the entrance. After they had burst into the terminal building, Feng steered Mac around a snaking line of customers wanting to buy tickets. Mac estimated that more than two hundred people waited in line, eating, talking on cell phones, complaining to their neighbor, tapping their feet, or just standing with vacant stares. A tone of resigned anxiety hung over the crowd.

The signs in the station were in Chinese and English, but the press of moving bodies made it impossible to stand long enough to read anything in detail. Mac decided he would never had been able to do this without Feng, who had given up a family evening to help him.

"This way," Feng shouted, grabbing Mac's hand. He followed as fast as he could, dragging the uncooperative suitcase behind them. She threaded him through queues of people waiting for trains, for bao, for coffee, for reading material. Grand Central Station at rush hour looked like the open prairies compare to this.

"The fast train to Shanghai always leaves from platform twelve. It's not worth trying to look at the schedule board." She pointed to an ocean of passengers clustered around an electronic board visible hundreds of meters away. "We'll barely make it to the train in time even if we go there directly."

Mac's train left at 1:09. The clock now read 12:55. He followed her as they slid their way through clusters of passengers. "Business class is at the front of the train," Feng said as they arrived at platform twelve. They headed for the first cars in the sequence. "We've done great. We actually have ten minutes to spare."

"Wait a minute." Feng stopped short and stared at the electronic sign in the carriage window. Mac bumped into her as she muttered, "Must be some mistake." She turned. "Stay here."

Mac stood with his bag battered by passersby, hoping that Feng remembered where she left him. He looked at his watch. 12:58. If he did not make the train he might be stranded in Wuhan for months.

Feng reappeared shaking her head. "The attendant says the tracks were switched. This train is going to Beijing. Ours is on track 21."

Mac stared at the waves of people buffeting him and his own exhausted body with aches in every muscle fiber. He still felt weak from his recovery, and the sprinting had left him without any reserve.

"I don't think I can make it," he said.

"Yes you can." She grabbed his suitcase and began to run, dragging it behind her. She zagged and zigged around passengers, staying as close as possible to the edge of the platform. At one point the bag slipped between the platform and carriage, almost pulling her onto the tracks. With a panicked look, Mac steadied her, grabbed the bag, and headed away from the platform edge.

The best option now was to wedge though the crowd. Mac took the lead, pushing his bag ahead of him like a ship's prow, twisting and torquing it to break through the masses.

Something happened that he had experienced in tense moments in surgery but never outside the operating room. Time slowed. His anxiety rolled away, replaced by a sense of peace. He felt as if someone else was driving. "I'll handle this. Don't worry," the voice in his head said.

Mac had lost most of his religious faith, but he did whisper "Thanks" as they arrived at Platform 21. It was five past one. The train left in four minutes.

"Thank God you have a business-class seat," Feng said, panting with effort. "The business car is up front, but it may take ten minutes to get to it. Get on the train now, then look for your seat by walking through the train cars."

She pushed him toward the nearest open door. The funnel effect of dozens of people trying to get through one door created a vortex. People lining up on the sides got peeled off and had to get back in line. Feng steered Mac to the center of the queue and pushed hard against the person in front. The force of others helped push him through.

At 1:08, Mac hauled his bag onto the car and pushed into the aisle. Feng remained behind, stepping out of the queue as the final whistle blew and a hundred doors along the train slammed shut. Travelers who had not gotten on snapped back as the train started moving. Some passengers just through the doorway looked mournfully at companions still shouting on the platform.

Mac got as close to a window as he could and mouthed thank you. Feng waved back with a triumphant smile on her face and disappeared as the train picked up speed and slid out of the station.

The carriage was packed with citizens of Wuhan of every age. All of them wore masks. The narrow central aisle had just enough space to allow Mac's bag to maneuver, with the occasional passenger blocking the way. The lighting was so low he could barely see where he was going, and the clicking of the rails provided a continuing counterpoint to his journey.

The air smelled stale, scented with sweat, garlic, and other odors Mac could not identify. Some passengers talked energetically, but most closed their eyes or sat looking straight ahead without speaking. The lurching and swaying of the train made each step a challenge.

When he arrived at glass doors proclaiming business class, he opened them and took a deep breath. For a few seconds he surveyed the tranquil scene, contrasting it with the chaos he had just left behind. Large armchairs placed a discrete distance from each other dotted the cabin. No narrow aisle here. With the fragrances of leather and expensive cologne filling the air, he thought he could be in a social club in Boston. His heart rate slowed and his tense muscles relaxed.

He showed his electronic ticket to the porter and followed the man to a large, comfortable seat. For the first time in several days, he felt at ease. He plugged his phone into a charging outlet, flattened the seat to create a bed, pulled two blankets over his body, and plunged immediately into stage four sleep.

He did not waken until the train pulled into Shanghai's Hongqiao station at five that morning. In darkness, he transferred by metro to the Longyang station. The transfer and subsequent boarding of the Maglev magnetic levitation train to Pudong International Airport flashed through his consciousness like a hazy dream. Only when he watched the former rice flats of Pudong rip past at 437 kilometers an hour did he realize he was truly on his way.

As always, Shanghai's airport, forty-five kilometers from the city, astounded him with its dazzling design and sheer size. Terminal One resembled an enclosed city more than an airport. Soaring white roofs with exposed beams in graceful elliptical curves brought to mind the set of a futuristic movie. Transparent walls with criss-crossed steel, spotless tile floors, and the rising sun seared the scene into his memory.

Although thousands of passengers rushed along its capacious innards, their footsteps and conversations were swallowed up in the size and soundproofing design. Planes came and went with almost no sound. The air smelled fresh, and there was none of the frantic tone of Wuhan.

A few people wore masks. No one wore gloves. There were some soldiers at the entrance, but their presence was less prominent than it had been in the Wuhan train station. The sense of a mass exodus that had characterized the Wuhan departure was nowhere to be seen here. This was just another Wednesday in a Chinese city of twenty-five million.

The check-in process flowed without incident, with no questions about his activities in China. The direct flight to Boston departed at 6:15 p.m., giving him most of the day to explore the airport.

He breezed through passport control and headed for the business class lounge. There he FaceTimed Lauren to say he was on schedule. He called up the Zhongnan Hospital website to see if there was important news. The case load had not changed. His lectures were highlighted on videos on the site.

He browsed the English newspapers, noting the US president's claim that he and his administration had the outbreak totally under control. Finally, he slept for two hours in the lounge's meditation room. He still felt shaky. After a long walk to the gate, he boarded the plane feeling as though he had stepped out of a nightmare.

His COVID-19 baptism had ended. He could not wait to see his family in person again.

He had a new mission in his professional life—to convince his fellow Americans that they faced a devastating enemy in the coronavirus, and that they needed to get ready for its attack.

He wasn't sure whether they, especially the federal administration, would listen.

CONFIRMATION

CHAPTER THIRTEEN

QUARANTINE IN BOSTON

JANUARY 24-28, 2020
BOSTON, MA

Mac slept fitfully for most of the flight, delighted to hear the announcement that they would land in Boston in twenty minutes. He arrived grateful that his hospital had refused to see him for a month. He would not have been able to provide anything like the care his patients needed.

He wondered whether questions about coronavirus infection would cause him to be detained at Logan immigration despite his Global Entry status.

The process was as easy as it always had been.

"Been away on business?" the border official asked.

"Yes."

"What field are you in?"

"I'm a surgeon."

"Welcome home, doctor."

He passed through the customs hall, obtained his bag, and exited into the arms of his tearful wife. "I said not to come," he said, realizing how much he had missed her.

"You think I'm going to let a virus keep me from welcoming my husband home?" she said. "I did leave the children at school, though."

"Believe me, the danger's not exaggerated. I'm still going to Julia's brother-in-law's condo for a couple of days until I know I'm safe."

"I can drive you there."

Mac felt intense relief watching the tunnels and highways of his familiar city flash by. Lauren chatted about her teaching, the children's schoolwork, and the situation in Boston. Nothing had changed. It was if the viral threat did not exist.

They found a parking place on Dartmouth St. and he settled into the one-bedroom first floor condominium. He and Lauren made a pact to FaceTime before school each morning and after dinner each evening.

He left a voicemail with his own doctor's office to set up an appointment, then called Russ Baxter at the CDC. "I'm back in Boston. but I want to track this virus's spread. I would like to have access to your CDC websites, the ones ordinary citizens can't reach."

"No problem. You're a special consultant and will get what you need from us. How are you feeling?"

"Still rough. My thinking is better, but my co-ordination is off and I'm exhausted all the time."

"Talking to someone who has been through this really makes a difference. I had no idea this was such a debilitating infection."

By midnight Mac had on his computer information from the equivalent of the CDC in every major country. His ability to log into Johns Hopkins epidemiology helped particularly. He was ready to watch the progress of a plague.

January 24, 2020
From: Dmacgregor@harborhospital.org
To: Russell.Baxter@CDC.gov
Topic: Update

Hi Russell:

I'm self-isolating in Boston. You will become more familiar with self-quarantining in the next few weeks. I have set up the computer and television feeds I need to be informed on COVID-19.

Here is a summary of the situation as I see it.

The virus is spreading. Singapore, Thailand, Japan, South Korea, Nepal, Australia, Malaysia, Cambodia, and Sri Lanka in Asia; and France and Germany in Europe, have all reported documented cases. I am sure you are aware of the first cases in the USA and Canada on the weekend. Some of these involve contacts with travelling Chinese, but some have no such interactions. They may come through Europe.

In Wuhan, cases were increasing exponentially last week. My friends in Wuhan public health calculated the R as 3-4. This virus seems to spread easily, person to person.

Extremely restrictive measures have been implemented to contain the infection. At ten a.m. yesterday, January 23, all commerce and transportation stopped in Wuhan. Stay-at-home orders enforced by the army. Masks and gloves for everyone. These restrictions will also be employed in other Hubei province cities.

Vietnam instituted a lockdown even earlier, recognizing that early containment is the only effective approach. Restrictive government action would be difficult to implement in the USA, but it is the only way to halt the progression of the disease.

Best,

Mac

Duncan MacGregor, MD, PhD, FACS, FAANS
Special Consultant to the Centers for Disease Control, USA
Director of the Brain Tumor Program, Harbor Hospital, Boston
Associate Professor of Neurosurgery, Harvard Medical School, Boston

January 26, 2020
From: Dmacgregor@harborhospital.org
To: Russell.Baxter@CDC.gov
Topic: Update

Hi Russell:

My colleagues in Wuhan tell me the lockdown is harsh in the extreme. Once a week a household member can leave to get groceries, but the grocery stores are running out of supplies. The streets are completely deserted. Perhaps the worst part of it is that no one knows how long all this will last. It is a solemn warning to us.

Three elements are vital as lessons for the United States when this hits us.

Definitive leadership willing to obey science. This cannot be a time to claim individual rights. Everyone in China understands that the health of each citizen depends on the health of the community as a whole.

Enough personal protective equipment for frontline workers, including doctors and nurses, to work safely. When the outbreak began, before we knew about the infectivity of the virus, many medical workers got exposed and got sick. We need to keep safe our front-line workers in medicine, in the army, in the police, in every other necessary service industry.

Testing to isolate and treat all components of disease spread.

Testing includes segregating out asymptomatic carriers, contacts of sick people, the sick patients themselves, and recovering patients. Wuhan has decided to build a new temporary hospital just for patients with this disorder. They say it will take less than two weeks. Sounds impossible to me, but we'll see.

The rest of China is dealing with the pressure too. Most airlines have suspended transit to and from China.

A quick side note. I don't know if you saw that Jack Ma, Alibaba's founder, has donated one hundred million Chinese yuan (that's fourteen million dollars) from his own foundation to further vaccine development. In the U.S., the Bill and Melinda Gates Foundation gave ten million dollars last week. Maybe private money will make things go faster, since we are certainly not seeing governmental funds being used well for this.

Best,

Mac

January 28, 2020
From: D.macgregor@harborhospital.org
To: Russell.Baxter@CDC.gov
Subject: consultant report

Russ:

This will be my last routine email. From your responses so far, I get the impression that you think this virus will be irrelevant for Americans because we are so far away from the source. I can't believe our president has said "We've pretty much shut it down." You haven't even begun to see what's going to happen. Don't be complacent about the imminent arrival of COVID-19. Even in Boston, the continuous roar of airplanes originating in Asia reminds me that, little by little, it is infiltrating even now. We have been given a grace period and should use it wisely.

The easy transmissibility and variable symptoms of this virus make it a huge public health hazard. We know it is spread person-to-person and **there are people now carrying the virus in the USA without symptoms.** Testing and contact tracing are keys to controlling the disease. The Beijing World Health meeting next week will have the facts to back this up.

Data scheduled to be published in two weeks will demonstrate that six percent of patients diagnosed with COVID-19 will need an ICU, three percent will require a ventilator, and one point four percent will die. All phases of the disease--asymptomatic carrier, ambulatory and hospitalized victim, ventilated patient, recovering patient, and corpse, need attention. Wuhan has been spectacular in anticipating the implications of these numbers for twelve million people, even building a three thousand bed hospital in ten days. That hospital has been packed since it opened.

Lockdowns have been effective in controlling the disease. Wuhan and fifteen neighboring cities have locked down fifty-seven million citizens. The resulting hardships are incredible, since people live in crowded conditions. How can we possibly do this in the US?

I know what is going to happen, but no one listens. We need to be sure we have enough test kits ready, have enough PPE for our hospitals and health care workers, and have leaders primed for the eventuality of lockdowns. I worry about the consequences for our country given the present political climate.

Best,

Mac

CHAPTER FOURTEEN

TESTING

MONDAY, FEBRUARY 3, 2020
BOSTON, MA

While Mac collected data on COVID-19, he also worked to get himself tested before participation in public events. He knew that the virus could persist in the nasal cavities of a patient long after clinical infection had passed, and did not want to become a spreader.

The problem was that the CDC guidelines did not allow asymptomatic patients to get tested. His own physician added that she could find no site that had test kits.

Mac decided to call the CEO of Harbor Hospital for an urgent appointment. Perhaps she could get test kits for staff.

"Impossible," the male administrative assistant said. "Dr. Renwick's fully booked for at least a month."

"I only need ten minutes."

"That's what everyone claims. No way she can accommodate you."

"Could you tell her it's Dr. Duncan MacGregor, and he wants to talk about COVID-19."

"I'll call you back after I talk with her."

"I'll wait on the line. I'd hate to miss your call."

He heard the annoyance in the man's voice and expected to be put on hold, then disconnected. Instead, he got a response almost immediately.

"She can see you in forty minutes."

"On my way," Mac answered. "And thanks!"

The CEO was a petite woman whose Givenchy suit complemented her pixie hairdo perfectly. Many associates had been fooled by her amiable manner and sparkling smile, not recognizing the intelligence and leadership that lay behind them. Mac had learned that underestimating her was a mistake.

Dr. Renwick greeted him with a smile but no handshake, invited him to sit on a chair placed several feet away from her desk. He noted again the Ph.D. diploma in psychology displayed behind her desk.

"It's nice to see you again, Mac. I trust Lauren and the family are well. I understand you had a difficult time in Wuhan. Is this meeting about getting back to work earlier than we suggested?"

"No."

"Great, because I was the one who decided you needed at least a month away. Some of my Shanghai colleagues report that the virus can linger in a patient's nostrils for four weeks. I don't want you to become part of our problem."

"Can't you test for virus? That's what I wanted to see you about. Isn't that something we need to offer?"

"Absolutely. And until this morning, I would say it couldn't be done. There are almost no test kits in the US, a fact that's hard to believe. I pleaded with my Shanghainese colleagues to help, and a shipment of a thousand kits just arrived. I'll put your name on one of them. Anything else?"

"Would you consider hosting a meeting of Boston hospital leaders to get ready for the virus's arrival here?"

"It's a great idea, but with everyone's schedule, it may take months to arrange."

"I suggest we do it virtually, with you as the moderator. We can use Zoom to get our participants all together at, say, noon Friday. They can join the session from their offices. It doesn't matter whether the hospital is represented by their top leader, although having you host will probably assure that most CEO's show up."

She looked at the far wall, a habit Mac had learned meant she was considering something carefully. "Would it be alarmist to call it so early? Boston has had only two COVID-19 cases—a student from Wuhan and one from Italy. They were reported ten days ago and seem to be recovering. No big outbreak."

"Believe me, the outbreak's coming. As a medical community we have to prepare psychologically and physically. We need masks and hats and gowns and ventilators, but more important we have to realize it will be a long fight."

"OK, I'll get you tested and arrange the conference if you'll do something for me."

"Which is?"

"Give a talk to the hospital community on your experiences with the virus. We can't depend on our national leadership to guide us with this pandemic. I don't want any patient to die here because we are unprepared. You'd be a perfect person to educate and energize us."

"When would this be?"

"On Thursday at our five o'clock interdisciplinary hospital rounds."

"That's just three days away."

"Can you do it?"

"Absolutely."

To get his test, Mac had to go to the Urgent Care waiting room. He felt foolish sitting among patients with real problems—swollen ankles, twisted limbs, wheezing, cuts and bruises.

In half an hour he was taken back to an examining room. The doctor did a doubletake when she entered, almond eyes bright behind her mask. "Dr. MacGregor! I'm Sheila Wu. You won't remember me, but my neurosurgical elective almost convinced me to do neurosurgery. My husband talked me out of it."

She continued, her warm energy making Mac smile. "And you had COVID-19? My family is in Shanghai. They say the situation in Hubei province is improving medically, but terrible for the people who are under quarantine."

She listened to a brief version of his story, took his temperature, checked his throat, listened to his chest. "No fever or chest abnormality." She extracted a long swab from her kit. "Look up, please."

The pain that followed made Mac realize that widespread testing might be a bigger problem than he thought.

An initial tickle as the swab entered his nostril turned into agony as the probe went deeper.

"We have to get it back to the nasopharynx," she said.

Mac twisted his head away involuntarily and could feel blood trickling down his right nostril. As Dr. Wu pulled the swab out, Mac sneezed with tears in his eyes, spraying blood onto his hand and shirt. He missed her only because he had turned to the side. He took out a tissue and pressed it against his right nostril to stop the nosebleed. "That was fun," he said.

"We don't want a false negative test because I didn't get back far enough," she said. "Sorry it was uncomfortable. I'll send the phlebotomist to get the blood for the antibody test. We'll have the results by tomorrow afternoon."

CHAPTER FIFTEEN

RESISTANCE

FEBRUARY 4-6, 2020
BOSTON, MA

Late the next afternoon, Mac got the information he had hoped for. His nasopharyngeal swab showed no active virus and his antibody titer was high, suggesting that he was resistant to further attack by this virus. He felt like a man released from prison.

He left for his Brookline home as soon as he got the news. Arriving, he opened the front door as quietly as he could, crept to the kitchen, and watched for a few seconds as Peter and Maggie scarfed down spaghetti. The babble of their excited conversation and the smell of pasta sauce trumpeted that he was truly home.

"That food looks good," he boomed. "Could I have some?"

His son and daughter raced to him, encircling his waist with their arms. Lauren planted a kiss on his cheek and hugged him, resting her head on his chest.

"We missed you ssooooo much," Maggie said.

"You don't look too sick," Peter said.

"What can I get you?" Lauren asked, rubbing her hand on his stubbled cheek.

"That beautiful smile is all I need."

The next day whirled with activity. Mac reviewed mail at the hospital and met with Dr. Pedroza about his patients. She assured him they had survived his absence and added that the hospital staff were all abuzz about his lecture. An annex room had been added to accommodate the anticipated demand.

Back at home, he could not resist his piano. The Bach Italian concerto, Beethoven Pathetique Sonata, and Brahms Opus 119 intermezzi issued clumsily from his fingers, reminding him how much he had missed the music he loved.

He worked at his lecture for an hour, then took a walk along Beacon Street. Snow still lay in clumps on the lawn and garden beds, but the sky was blue and the cold air refreshed him. The sounds of quiet traffic, songs of a few birds, and sight of neighbors going about their business lessened his anxiety and made him grateful to be home again. He wondered how much would change when the virus arrived.

At his five o'clock lecture, people of all ages and departments packed the auditorium as he began. Some were familiar, including his own students and faculty. Dr. Renwick, hospital leadership, Dr. Pedroza, and neurosurgical staff sat in the front two rows.

Most attendees were unknown to him.

In the lecture, Mac described the effect of the virus on Wuhan, his own experiences, and the implications for the future in the US. At the end, he had to stop a standing ovation to invite questions.

A man with perfectly combed brown hair, starched white shirt, silk tie, and brown suit moved to the microphone.

"Dr. MacGregor, thank you for his vivid presentation," he said. "Really, though, aren't you just talking about the flu, not some bizarre new virus? Nothing new about influenza, is there? We know it is a serious illness that kills thirty thousand Americans a year. Those Chinese probably just don't know what they're looking at."

"Excuse me?" Mac was caught off guard so completely he did not know what to say.

The man turned to the audience and swung the microphone in front of him with a practiced move. "I said, this is just a form of the same old influenza. How many people here have had the flu?"

About a third of the audience shot their hands in the air.

"You see. It's that season. You happened to get a severe form in Wohan or whatever that city was."

"And you are?"

"You don't recognize me? Doesn't everybody watch Right TV? I'm Barker Marsden from the Marsden Report. Anybody here ever see my show?" He scanned the auditorium, completely taking command with his good looks and a suit that could have been an advertisement for a bespoke tailor shop.

A few members of the audience applauded; most hissed.

"Mr. Marsden, do you realize the molecular analysis of the virus shows it's completely different than flu?" Mac asked.

"Those tests don't mean a thing. Why, I could probably show you twenty foreign viruses in your nose. Doesn't mean they're causing any trouble."

"I don't think you understand—"

"Now let me just ask you one small question, Dr. MacGregor. Did you get your flu shot this year?"

"No, but—"

Marsden raised his arms like a preacher calling on the lord. "You see, you have here a doctor who doesn't get a flu shot, gets the Asian flu, and wants to rile us all up about some newfangled virus. I suggest you take better care of yourself next time, Doctor. Why are you hiking off to places like China anyway? Now excuse me, I have a plane to catch."

He strutted out of the auditorium.

CHAPTER SIXTEEN

HOSPITAL CEOs

FEBRUARY 6-7, 2020
BOSTON, MA

Mac trembled with anger as the newscaster left. The hospital CEO joined him at the podium to say formal thank you for the presentation, suggesting with a smile that the hospital should check for hijackers before starting future lectures.

"Thanks for your comments about hijacking, but what was that interruption really about?" Mac asked her privately as the audience dispersed. "Was that guy just stupid, or was he deliberately misleading us?"

Dr. Renwick's smile faded. "This was no accident, Mac. You have just witnessed the new propaganda machine. I've been talking with colleagues elsewhere in the country, and it's a big problem."

"They would sabotage a hospital grand rounds?"

She nodded. "They'll try to block any attempt to provide information that contradicts their party line. We believe in truth and science. I take some credit for promoting that culture here. The proponents of the new reality think their fantasy can overcome truth."

"But this was just an educational lecture."

"It violated the party line promoted by the president and the flunkies around him, so they sent one of their spokesmen to sow doubt and confusion. This is happening everywhere around the country."

"You mean this was deliberate falsification?"

"Oh yes. They don't have to give data to support their alternative reality, just keep saying it exists."

"Excuse me?"

"The Washington administration seems committed to denying COVID-19 as a reality."

"But how is that possible? Don't they realize the implications for the country? Thousands, maybe hundreds of thousands, of preventable deaths."

"I know that and you know that. With the conservative media downplaying the dangers, there's not much we can do nationwide. We can have the hospitals of Boston ready for the onslaught. Thank you for presenting your story. I will support whatever you can do to keep our attention on the health crisis that's coming."

"The lecture was great," Lauren said as they drove home together later that night, "and I wouldn't worry about Barker Marsden. He has his own talk show, but he just defends the administration's position on everything. He's only a legend in his own mind."

"Why would he bother to come to my lecture?"

"I saw in the Globe that he was getting an award from

the Young Conservatives Club today. Probably thought he would just stop by and sow some discord. I don't have to tell you that the president has minimized coronavirus. Marsden is just a mouthpiece."

Later that evening, Lauren called Mac over to the television.

"It's a press conference the president is giving on COVID," she said. Mac watched, incredulous, as the leader of the United States claimed that COVID-19 was a hoax, a ploy by the Democrats to unseat him. He went on to say that at a Boston hospital earlier tonight a doctor claimed to have experienced coronavirus infection when he probably just had the flu. Of course, this leftist physician had been in China and probably had been brainwashed there—or needed his brains washed to go there in the first place.

"Those Right TV people must have a direct line to the president," Mac said.

"I think that's where he gets his information and advice. That's why I watch them regularly. The network mouths the party line, so I know what to expect from the White House. One host in particular—names Melody Swift—seems to have his ear. Sad, really. I don't even know if he ever reads anything. Some Right TV news people are closer to the president than his advisers."

Mac shook his head. He hoped the hospital CEOs he had lined up for the meeting the next day would understand the COVID-19 situation better.

At the appointed time, the leaders of ten Boston hospitals logged into Zoom with Dr. Renwick as moderator.

Mac started the discussion with an account of his stay in China, the terrible experience of having COVID-19, the aftermath of exhaustion which he still felt, and his service on the Wuhan mayor's committee. "To sum up," he said, "The devastation of this virus is hard to imagine if you haven't experienced it yourself. And we must prepare for it here."

A microbiologist from the MGH spoke next, describing coronaviruses in general and the emerging understanding of their spread. They could be passed from person to person, and early data suggested the new coronavirus combined the easy infectivity of the common cold with the severity of SARS, making it a formidable opponent.

The next lecture patched them into the Wuhan public health department through the hospital's telemedicine facility. Mac felt he was back in China when he saw the epidemiologist. She described how tracing and isolation of contacts to identify potential carriers had been necessary, along with a strict lockdown, to control the infection.

At that point, one participant from the Boston hospitals interrupted. "All this just shows inept management of a public health hazard by the Chinese. China needs to get its health system together. This virus will never affect us." He signed off, but the others continued as if nothing had happened.

The conference ended with a report from Northeastern University. Using mathematical modeling, researchers there showed that already in the United States there were more than a thousand carriers of the virus spreading throughout the country. Challenged about where these 'Typhoid Marys' could be found, the speaker said. "Look around you. Any of the people you see could be a carrier. Some will be asymptomatic because the infection is early. Some will never get sick. Some are sick but think it's just a cold."

Dr. Renwick closed the conference with the simple statement that lives would be lost if the hospitals did not take COVID-19 seriously. The participants agreed to form a coalition to be prepared for the safe treatment of patients when the tidal wave hit.

Mac said a quiet prayer of thanks. At least Boston hospitals would not take the onslaught lying down.

CHAPTER SEVENTEEN

SWIFT CURRENTS

FEBRUARY 13-18, 2020
NEW YORK, NY

A week after his lecture, Mac got a call from a woman named Melody Swift, who introduced herself as the host of *Swift Currents* on the Right TV network. She had heard he had personal experience with coronavirus and asked him to appear on her show to tell his story.

Mac's immediate inclination was to refuse, even though he didn't know the various network broadcast hosts.

He asked Lauren what she thought. "I agree it's risky," she said, "but it may be worth a try. I watch Melody's show regularly. She's a born-again Christian who's smart but always defends the administration's party line. She must have a rebel streak in her, because she never married but has an adopted daughter."

"Is there a chance she would listen to me?"

"It's worth a try, but there's a definite risk."

Mac looked Melody up on Linked-In. Thirty-six. Childhood in Virginia, college at Cornell. Started in CNN as a journalist, but gravitated to Right TV for "philosophical reasons." In her photo, intelligent eyes. A thin face not traditionally beautiful, but high cheekbones and aquiline nose making it memorable.

It appeared she was well-educated. Perhaps he could convince her to change her mind.

He decided to present a counter-proposal. "I'll appear on your show if three scientists and I can make a presentation to you about COVID-19 before it airs."

"Your COVID-19 piece is slotted for Monday. I won't have time to get up to Boston before then. I would be willing to watch your presentation the week after."

"That's OK with me. I want to convince you before it's too late that coronavirus is a real problem."

"Deal."

On February sixteenth, Mac started his visit to the Right TV studios by passing through Rockefeller Center. The morning sunlight glinted from the golden sculptures and highlighted the art deco skyscrapers. Skaters rounded the rink in random synchrony, united by the waltz music piped over the plaza. Scents of coffee and perfume wafted on warm air blasts from open shop doors, and the excited chatter of tourists mingled with the cacophony of morning traffic in midtown Manhattan.

Moving toward the Sixth Avenue, he had a sudden urge to turn around and go back to Boston. He desperately wanted to educate the public about COVID-19. But appearing on Right TV? Other networks like CNN, MSNBC, and NPR were more in his comfort zone.

It was that very challenge that drove him. Could he transform a likely opponent into a supporter? The stakes were high if he could, and he wanted to make a difference.

There was no mistaking the forty-five-story Right TV building as he approached it. Windows with R I G H T N E W S occupied street level, an electronic notice board with streaming headlines wrapped around the second floor, and giant portraits of personalities smiled from the third. Attractive men and women who looked as though they were modeling skin lotion and tailored suits streamed in and out of the building.

Among those men and women, Mac had no trouble identifying Melody. A little taller than the women around her, she stood at the entrance scanning the street, auburn hair blowing in the wind. Her face displayed flawless creamy skin and striking hazel eyes. A tailored alpaca coat and Burberry scarf wrapped around a slender body, complemented by high-heeled Louis Vuitton boots.

"Hi, Dr. MacGregor. Welcome to Right TV," Melody said, smiling and extending her hand as he approached. Her handshake was warm and firm. "We can have lunch in our dining room. I blocked out an hour before our official work begins."

As the elevator rose, Mac noted that the Wall Street Journal, New York Post, and Dow Jones were tenants in the same building as Right TV. Part of the same ideological empire too, he mused.

Melody led them to a reserved corner table. "I want to begin by saying thank you. Four years ago, you took care of my sister Janice when she had a malignant brain tumor."

"Janice Swift was your sister? I remember her well. She taught English at Lesley University. A lovely woman. Your parents were troupers through the whole ordeal."

"I watched from the sidelines. I was super busy trying to get things going here at Right TV and had my daughter to take care of. I also couldn't bear to go to the family meetings and hear about how soon my sister was going to die."

"It must have been tough on everyone."

Melody nodded. "My mom and dad never got over it. They were killed in a car accident two years ago. I'm the only one left to say thanks." She stopped and looked out the window. Her lips trembled a little.

"For what?"

"For you. The only bright spot in the whole experience was having you as her doctor. You were caring and competent and compassionate, and the team you led was wonderful. I never got around to writing, but when I heard about your COVID-19 story I thought this would be a great opportunity to meet and express my gratitude in person."

Mac felt from her a sincerity and warmth he was unprepared for. "I'm so sorry you had to go through all that," he said. "And thank you for your kind words. I'll convey them to my team, who are really the people responsible."

He looked out the window as well, as if trying to reconfigure what she had seen a few moments ago. He turned back to her with a hopeful smile. "Does that mean you'll be sympathetic to what I have to say today?"

She smiled back. "We learn in this business to separate personal from business lives. I'm still a Right TV host. Tell me about what happened to you in China."

Mac went through his experience, noting that she listened intently and seemed to absorb his main points. The hour went fast, accompanied by a delicious Cobb salad and lobster bisque. As their lunch finished, she said that the bulk of the time would be devoted to his own account, but she might ask a question or two. She emphasized that they only had three minutes of airtime together.

They proceeded to separate cubicles for makeup, then to the studio. There, the difference between the transmitted image and the reality of the set underlined for Mac the difference between the fantasy world of broadcasting and the real world.

The fantasy world showed a host sitting at a large desk with generous space around her.

The real world displayed a woman seated at a small plywood desk with cameras pivoting continually around her, guided by men in jeans. The room was too hot and too bright and too stuffy and smelled of electronics.

Melody looked perfectly cool in a navy-blue suit with a small American flag pin on her left lapel. She smiled at Mac and invited him to sit at the periphery of the shot until she was ready for him. Watching her talk about various news items, he contemplated the futility of compressing three weeks of his disease into three minutes that would convince viewers coronavirus was a threat.

Before they went live, she directed him to a seat beside the desk close enough to her to make him uncomfortable. Social distancing had become part of his norm. He moved his chair back to his comfortable six feet distance, especially since she forbade wearing a mask. She commented that getting host and guest in one camera shot provided a sense of intimacy that was important for viewers. "Your cameramen will just have to make it work," he said.

She did not have time to argue before the red light flashed on the camera. Turning toward it, she announced, "Welcome back. We have as a special guest tonight Professor Duncan MacGregor from Boston who has an up close and personal view of COVID-19 to share with us. Dr. MacGregor, welcome to *Swift Currents*."

In the monitor, Mac saw himself framed in the camera shot, smiling as he thanked her.

"You look great, Doctor, but I understand you experienced COVID-19 only a few months ago. Can you describe what happened?"

"I was a visiting professor in Wuhan when the pandemic began and I contracted coronavirus infection. I got extremely sick." He went on to summarize what had happened, uninterrupted for two minutes.

"How are you feeling now?"

"Getting better, but I still fatigue easily."

Melody looked away from Mac and directly at the camera. "Here is a man who came through this dreaded infection looking pretty darn good now. Perhaps this virus isn't so bad after all."

"Well, I can tell you it's—"

"Excuse me, but we don't have much time left and I wanted to ask one more quick question. We haven't had as many problems with this 'pandemic' as the third-world Chinese.

Isn't all the alarm about the coronavirus coming to America overstating the situation? We have better health, better medical care. We're just a greater country. Isn't this really just a problem for China?"

"Don't worry, it's going to come to America." Mac felt his body tighten as he got ready for the gist of the discussion.

"Well, doctor, we are so grateful to you for taking time out to talk with our viewers today. Thank you, and good luck in your work."

After the camera lights went off, Melody approached a stunned Mac. "Was that OK?"

"No," he said. "You cut me off before I could say what's important."

"I thought you did a great job. As for cutting you off, I let your story flow. I could have claimed what you had in China was the flu, or was only bad because you had terrible medical care. I told you we only had three minutes. Really scary what happened to you in Wuhan, though. I'm glad you made it."

"I don't think we conveyed the right tone," Mac said, still irritated. "I should have refused to come on the show."

"Everyone new to the broadcast game thinks they have been misrepresented. I think we had a good message. Our viewers should realize how bad this Chinese infection can be. I'm just glad it's not going to be a big problem here."

"But it is going to be a big problem. That's what I want to convince you about."

"You can try next week. And I'm going to try to persuade you it's all a hoax."

"It's no hoax. I know what this disease can and will do."

Mac felt more sad than angry as he walked out of the building. This was a well-educated, caring person. He liked her despite her political beliefs and realized the interview could in fact have been a lot worse. He just hoped she had enough flexibility to listen to what he and his colleagues had to say.

After MacGregor left, Melody felt unsure about what had just happened. She had pulled her punches. She could have run circles around him, left him looking and feeling ridiculous. In the past, she had never hesitated to make guests look bad if she disagreed with their politics.

She liked Duncan MacGregor, and he had truly made her sister's illness tolerable those many years ago. He did not seem to care about appearances or spinning a story in a certain way. He spoke with the power of sincerity. Barker Marsden had not done him justice when he boasted about interfering with MacGregor's lecture at Harbor Hospital. Dr. MacGregor was a good person.

She was not sure who would convince whom when they met next week in Boston.

CHAPTER EIGHTEEN

TUTORIAL

MARCH 2-3, 2020
BOSTON, MA

To keep her appointed meeting with Mac and his colleagues, Melody decided a three-hour car ride from her Greenwich home would get her to Boston faster than rail or plane. She would drive up and back the same day.

On Monday, she taped Tuesday's show and let her daughter Emily know she would be out of town. Early Tuesday morning, she headed north in her Lexus hybrid SUV. By one p.m., she was strolling along Boston's harbor walk, wind whipping through her hair, puffer jacket wrapped securely around her, salty air of the Atlantic Ocean invigorating her lungs.

Feeling refreshed and alive, she joined Mac and his colleagues in a Harbor Hospital conference room.

Mac introduced everyone. "Melody Swift, meet our virologist, Dr. Linda Watkins, from the medical school, Dr Victor Karpov, our epidemiologist from the school of public health, and Dr. Julia Pedroza, a neurosurgeon here at Harbor Hospital."

They took their places at a conference table in front of a projector screen. "Thanks for coming," Mac said. "We wanted to give you our scientific understanding of COVID-19. Dr. Watkins will start us off."

Watkins, a fifty-something woman with intense brown eyes, projected onto the screen a molecule that looked like a landmine with a coiled spring inside it.

"This is Sars-Cov2, the virus that causes COVID-19. Its method of operation is simple. It attaches to a human cell, drills a hole in the membrane, and pumps RNA into the center. As you know, RNA or ribonucleic acid is the template cells use to make protein. The viral RNA hijacks the cell's manufacturing system and codes it to make new virus. With its innards replaced with virus, the cell explodes and releases millions of new virus particles to destroy the cells around it."

She followed with a slide that looked like an arrowhead. "This is the hook the virus uses to latch onto the cell. It targets a particular receptor on the surface of cells in our nose, windpipe, and lungs."

"What's a receptor?" Melody asked, more to humor Mac than to get information. The question would prove she was listening.

"You can think of it as a doorway on the cell membrane that opens with a specific key. The virus has that key."

Melody thought a moment. "What if the virus developed a master key?"

"That is a disaster scenario we don't want to consider. In brief, the body would die from massive infection."

"And why doesn't it do that anyway?" Melody was

enjoying this presentation now. Sort of like a puzzle being put together piece by piece.

"The body sends its defender cells to kill virus particles. We have blood cells—T cells—that recognize the invader and attack it. They also help B cells produce antibodies. These antibodies form complexes with the viral coat and allow other white blood cells to eat it."

"Why don't antibodies attack the coronavirus from the start?" Melody asked.

"That's the main problem with this virus. Humans have not been exposed to it before, so most of us lack antibodies to clean it up. A few of us probably have them by chance, however. Those fortunate few become carriers who can spread the virus without becoming sick."

"Do you get antibodies after you've been infected?"

"Yes."

"Couldn't we give those to prevent infection in other people?" Melody leaned forward, fully engaged now.

Mac interrupted with a grin of approval. "You're quite an immunologist, Melody. Yes. Some scientists suggest it would be a good stopgap measure until we get a vaccine."

"And what does a vaccine do?"

"Trains the body to produce its own antibodies," Dr. Watkin said, "by giving a weak form of the virus. That way a person doesn't have to borrow antibodies from someone else."

"One more question for Dr. Watkins, and then we'll move on," Mac said. "Is this virus like the flu?"

"Definitely not," Watkins said. "Saying coronavirus and

the flu are the same is like saying a dog and a wolf are identical. They're totally different creatures."

"Thank you," Mac said. "Can we hear about epidemiology now?"

Dr. Karpov took his place beside the screen. "In evolution, this virus developed in bats, and is therefore totally new to humans."

"Yes, and all this happened because the Chinese eat bats. Disgusting!" Melody said.

"I'm sorry, but you're wrong. We don't think spread by eating contaminated food is likely. It is certainly not the usual way of passing virus. All the infections we see come from airborne particles spread from one human to another. We think as many as forty percent of people in a population exposed to coronavirus will become symptomatic, ten percent will require hospitalization, and one and a half percent will die."

"Isn't our death rate really low?" Melody said.

"Yes," Karpov replied, "but that has nothing to do with the spread of virus. It describes the number of infected people who ultimately die. The death rate reflects the skill of doctors and hospitals, not the virus itself."

"So what does describe the virus's spread?" Mac asked.

"These curves do." Karpov flashed slides with curves showing rising infection in every major country. "They all have one thing in common. Every country shows exponential increases until extreme restrictive measures are taken."

"That's because the countries don't have good health care." Melody's voice had less bravado. Those curves were impressive. She began to worry. *Is the USA just starting its burden of infection? Will the virus hit hard in a few months?*

"Wrong again about the health care," Karpov said. "Health care may change how many infected patients die, but has nothing to do with how many people get infected in the first place. That depends on the ability and willingness of government to take restrictive measures against the virus."

"Whatever you say, but it's not likely to infect someone like me," Melody crowed.

"Three strikes and you're out," Karpov said, apparently taking pleasure in disproving Melody. "I spend a lot of time trying to get people like you to realize the virus will come for them too. It's just going to happen later than in Hispanics or Blacks or old people."

Melody stood and began to wag her finger at the epidemiologist. "You have no idea what you're talking about. Just because a bunch of Chinese peasants living under terrible conditions get infected doesn't mean the virus is going to come to Greenwich Connecticut."

Mac stepped in to stop what looked like it might become a physical fight. "I think we should wrap this up, but I believe Dr. Karpov is correct. The infection will spread to involve everyone. We only have one more speaker. Dr. Pedroza will talk about the effect of COVID-19 on the body."

Pedroza did not use slides. "This disease affects the lungs mainly, but it can involve the heart, brain, kidneys, skin, and gastrointestinal tract as well. Sometimes the body's own defenses become the problem and the virus sets off a massive immune response."

"You mean the body starts to attack itself?" Melody asked.

"Yes, and that reaction can be more fatal than the infection."

"How do we prevent that?"

"By preventing the disease. Social distancing, masks, testing."

Mac asked, "Julia, can you comment on the implications of COVID-19 for what we call front-line workers?"

"Absolutely," Pedroza said. "Those workers include firefighters, EMT technicians, police officers, meat packing workers, grocery store clerks, all the people who have to face the public day after day. They need to have good protective equipment, especially masks, and use disinfectants on surfaces touched by others."

"How about health care workers?" Mac asked.

"It applies especially to them, since some of their patients are bound to have COVID-19."

"And hospitals?"

"Hospitals need to be prepared by testing, storing enough protective equipment for doctors, having excellent intensive care including enough ventilators, and arranging somewhere for recovering patients to do rehabilitation."

"We already have the best health care system in the world," Melody said.

"The simple fact is that our hospitals are not prepared for three things because of the federal administration's denial of the problem."

"But—"

Pedroza interrupted Melody to continue. "And the problem goes beyond hospitals. We also need places to isolate asymptomatic people who test positive. We are going to see real trouble if we don't start making these arrangements now. And there seems no interest in the federal administration to do this."

Melody found the discussion impossible. The implications of the problem were simply too great to take in. Sometimes you just had to block your mind to what is happening.

She stood and looked at her watch. "I have to get back on the road to make it back to Greenwich before the rush hour. Thanks for the presentation." She walked out, leaving the presenters sitting with puzzled expressions.

Once she got on the road, Melody lost the arrogant demeanor she had adopted during the presentation. Although she tried to maintain stubborn adherence to the Republican party line, the talks upset her. What if she were wrong and Mac and his colleagues were right?

She was worried by the image of the virus, by those infection curves, by the apparent lack of action by the government. There could be a lot of trouble ahead.

CHAPTER NINETEEN

THE BRONX

MARCH 16-20, 2020
THE BRONX, NY

Mac returned work as soon as his month of enforced leave finished. He asked to devote only half-time to neurosurgery because his energy was still limited, and he wanted to continue his efforts against the coronavirus.

He noted with relief that Boston at this time still only had a trickling of cases, and they were all in students who had been in China. Seattle had a cluster which was traced to one traveler. Towns north of Milan in Italy had a substantial outbreak.

Then there was the Bronx. Initially hidden in the back pages of the national papers, the growth of COVID-19 in the northern borough of New York City escalated in March.

Ramon, one of Mac's former residents, called him out of the blue in mid-March.

"Mac, I hear you know a lot about the management of COVID-19 patients. I'm chief medical officer of the Bronx Municipal Hospital now. We can't do any elective neurosurgery because we're seeing an uptick in COVID-19 cases. We could use your advice on a bunch of issues. Could you come down as visiting professor for a couple of days?"

Mac wanted to help, but consulted with Lauren first. Their family life had returned to normal, and he did not want to disrupt it. "I should only be gone three days, and it may save some lives."

"Are you in any danger of getting sick again?"

"No. I know I have antibodies to the virus and certainly will take the precautions I need."

"Will you promise three days maximum? I'm worried about my father and I might need you to visit him with me. He says one of the people in his senior living facility came down with COVID-19. Dad's fine, but it would be good to know you're here if there's trouble."

"It's only a four-hour drive to the Bronx."

"What about the children—could you spread it to them?"

"Someone with immunity does not become a carrier."

"Let me think about it for a while."

The next morning, Lauren gave her blessing. "I know how much fighting this virus means to you. Go, but please be careful."

Mac piled into his SUV and drove to the Bronx Municipal Hospital.

Ramon met him at the door. "Thanks so much for coming down. We don't have any N95 masks left. This may give some protection." He handed Mac a single thickness cotton fabric mask and they picked their way through dozens of men and women, mostly Hispanic and Black, crowding the corridors.

"I never dealt with anything like this before," Ramon said. "Our intensive care unit is overwhelmed. We've been trying to get ventilators from other hospitals in the region, but they're reluctant to send them. They anticipate the same problem happening in their hospitals in the near future. Even if we get ventilators, we don't have the staff trained to take care of this number of patients with this much respiratory trouble."

Mac met with the nursing and medical staff in a conference room stuffed with excess equipment moved from patient areas. Questions about the transmission of the disease, the natural course of infection, his own experiences, and the Wuhan management bombarded him. Many of the workers had large families. One of their first questions was whether they were already taking the virus from the hospital to the community.

Mac presented the importance of wearing a mask, minimizing direct contact with patients, using good handwashing procedures, and isolating anyone with symptoms.

"Have you seen our houses?" one nurse's aide asked. "It's impossible to keep separate from others."

"Not only that, but we don't have any masks to wear," another said.

"And we are a community. We care about each other, so the idea of sitting in isolation just doesn't click with us."

"Can you get tested?" Mac asked.

"Not at all. We can't get test kits," Ramon answered. "As far as I know, no one can."

Mac realized now the enormity of the problem. In China, the government understood that the virus must be contained no matter what the social inconvenience. In the United States, the federal administration had wasted the month of February denying and minimizing the impact of the plague. With the freedom of travel and of individual discretion, the infection had already spread throughout the country. The Bronx was only the start. It was just a matter of time for the rest of America to fall.

In the evening, Mac joined haggard nurses and doctors watching presidential briefings. As the country's leader claimed there was no big problem with COVID-19, they watched death wagons haul away their daily load of corpses.

Their situation began to gain national attention. Ramon announced that several television networks would be sending crews over the next few days.

The day after Mac arrived in the Bronx, Melody Swift appeared, surrounded by Right News videocams.

"We meet again, Ms. Swift," he shouted over the cluster of patients between them.

"Dr. McGregor! What a pleasant surprise!" Her smile and greeting seemed genuine. "What are you doing so far away from Boston?"

"I came down to help. I hope what you see here convinces you that this virus is a serious problem."

"All I see is a hospital poorly equipped to take care of its patients. Why can't they put more staff here and why weren't they better prepared?"

Mac moved toward her. "They have been unable to get the resources they need from the government. It's a mess. Would you like to see what's going on behind the scenes?"

He tried to hide the anger and scorn in his voice. If he could convince her, perhaps she could get the message across to the country and influence the president.

"This is what it is," she said, spreading her arms as if she were showing piles of garbage.

"I want you to see what goes on in parts of the hospital reporters don't get to visit."

Her eyes lit up. "You could do that?"

"I think I can. You can't bring a camera, but I think I can arrange it."

Fifteen minutes later, wrapped in an operating room gown, boots, hat and mask, Melody picked her way through dozens of patients packed into operating rooms, ICU's, corridors, sometimes two to a bed.

"This is certainly awful, but all it shows is poor preparation," Melody said.

"How can a hospital prepare for ten times as many patients as it is built for? And why didn't the federal administration transmit the knowledge that this was coming? They knew it from the experience in China and Italy."

"I think these people would be victims of any disease that came along. They live so close together and—"

"Are you saying it's their fault they're sick? That because they don't have resources to live in big separate homes, they deserve to die? Is that what you were implying?" Mac could not hide the irritation in his voice.

Melody did not answer. Mac continued, "And what about the medical personnel on the front lines here—doctors, nurses, nurse's aides, technicians. Why do they not have the equipment they need? We live in the United States, a manufacturing giant. The administration has the ability to mandate production of protective equipment. Why are our health care workers without the protection that will make them safe?"

"I think we have manufactured more than enough masks and all that stuff," Melody replied. "I don't even know if they are necessary. And maybe nurses are re-selling some of the personal protective equipment the state gives them. Perhaps that's why there are these shortages."

"Do you really believe that?"

"I think people are motivated by money and do all sorts of strange things."

Mac realized it was no use. He liked Melody personally, but she had blinders on which led to chronic denial. He had hoped the shock of seeing the conditions under which health care workers tried to cope with COVID-19 would change her mind. He now knew an entire shift in world view would be necessary.

She needed to see the world through entirely different eyes.

The president later that night wondered publicly whether health care workers were selling PPE on the street to make money rather than to help their colleagues.

For the exhausted nurses and doctors huddled around the television to get some hopeful news, that was the last straw. An EMT raced to the television, pulled the plug from the wall outlet, and cut it with his scissors. "Better to imagine we're alone trying to give care than watch this stuff," he said to a round of cheers.

Mac drove back to Boston the next morning, depressed by the conditions in the Bronx and angered by the refusal of the conservative press to recognize the travesty. He learned two facts. Melody Swift had access to the president that made her more important than any senator or head of government committee. And the United States was less able to deal with this virus than China was.

CHAPTER TWENTY

THE NURSING HOME

FRIDAY, MARCH 20, 2020
BOSTON, MA

"I need to visit my father. Can you help?" Lauren asked Mac the day he returned. "His senior living facility sent him to the hospital yesterday. They say he has a lung infection, but they couldn't test for coronavirus. He's at the Boston General. Can you get me in to see him?"

"I don't think so."

"What do you mean you don't think so. You're a big shot in Boston medicine. Can't you pull some strings?"

"The hospitals have closed down visiting."

"Can't I at least get in to wave at him through a window or something to make sure he knows I love him?"

"I'm sure he knows that. I'll call to see what I can do."

The Department of Health for Massachusetts confirmed a strict no visitation policy. Mac arranged for a Skype conversation instead of a visit.

The nurse set up a laptop computer on the over-the-bed table. Mac looked over Lauren's shoulder at a screen showing a gray-complexioned patient whose face was obscured by nasal prongs and an oxygen mask. Lauren repeatedly called her father's name. She got no response.

A doctor wearing a mask appeared and introduced himself. "Mrs. MacGregor, I believe we will have to intubate your father if he has any chance of survival. Do you wish us to go ahead with that procedure?"

Lauren looked at Mac. He nodded, and she said yes. "I'll call you back tomorrow morning to give an update," the doctor said and ended the call.

"What's going to happen. Mac? Does he have a chance?"

"The next twenty-four hours will tell."

The next morning the same doctor called. He showed Lauren's father behind him, intubated and unresponsive. "We're not having good luck," he said. "His lungs have filled with fluid, and his kidneys are showing signs of shutdown."

"Can you talk with my husband?" Lauren asked.

"This is Dr. Duncan MacGregor," Mac said as he faced the computer screen.

"Hi Dr. MacGregor. I know who you are. I'm Jim Coughlin, the respiratory ICU director. Your father-in-law has bilateral lung whiteouts on chest Xray and sats running seventy-five with twenty centimeters of PEEP. His BUN is fifty and creatinine had climbed to three. He's unresponsive to deep pain."

"Do you need a do-not-resuscitate order?"

"We're probably not going to save him even if we call a code, but a directive would help."

Mac turned to Lauren. "I'm so sorry. His lungs are full

of infection. I don't think he's going to make it through the day. The doctor wants to know if they can have an order not to resuscitate."

"Absolutely not. He's my father. I'm going to do everything I can for him."

"But everything probably won't help."

"Mac, he's my father. I don't care what you say. I'm not okaying anything but full treatment."

"I heard that," the voice from the computer said. "We'll keep him full code."

The final call from the same physician came at six the next morning. "I'm sorry to say your father has passed. His heart stopped about an hour ago and we couldn't get it started."

"Does this happen to all your patients with COVID-19?" Lauren shouted at the computer.

Dr. Coughlin remained calm. "No. Only about five percent. Your dad's Parkinson's Disease may have compromised his lungs."

"Then why did he die?"

Mac came up behind Lauren and interrupted, "I think that's enough, Lauren."

She turned away and began to cry. "I'm sorry. I do apologize. It's just so unfair. Dad lived eighty-two years, overcoming every obstacle including Parkinson's, and now a goddammed virus does him in. Can I see him before he goes to the morgue?"

"I'm sorry. No," Dr. Coughlin said. "Your husband will

tell you the rules. Is there anything else I can help with?"

"Thank you, no." Mac said, "except how come you're there so early?"

"We're doing double shifts. This COVID-19 situation is hitting us hard."

Lauren's anger doubled as she tried to make funeral arrangements for her father. *Ten people maximum*—that hardly accommodated her family. *Socially distanced*—no hugs, no crying on shoulders, no hand holding.

Masks throughout—like a group of bandits. *No open casket and no visitation*—no chance for friends and neighbors to say proper goodbye. *Cremation* only.

She looked at Mac with tears in her eyes after the service. "Could we have avoided this?"

"Perhaps, if our federal administration did its job."

CHAPTER TWENTY-ONE

THE FUNDRAISER

MARCH 22-23, 2020
WASHINGTON, D.C.

When Melody received an invitation to join the president's retinue at fundraising events for his largest donors, she usually accepted with delight.

When his executive secretary called this time, Melody looked for excuses not to go. In the past she'd been flattered and proud to be seen with him and count herself part of his faithful inner group.

COVID-19 was not an issue then. After the discussion with Mac's group and the devastation she saw in the Bronx, she worried that she might bring the coronavirus back to her daughter, Emily.

She knew only too well the backslapping, whisper-in-the-ear atmosphere of these events. She knew most of the men would not consider wearing a mask, and sometimes the suggestions they whispered in her ear were not pleasant.

She explained to the executive secretary that she might not be able to attend.

Ten minutes later the president himself called her. "I hear you might not make it to the fundraiser tomorrow night," he said in a tone that implied she was about to commit a terrible crime.

"Yes sir. I've been trying to catch up on a bunch of things, including time with my daughter."

"You know who this is, don't you?"

"Yes, Mr. President."

"I certainly hope you won't disappoint me. I look forward to seeing you at seven sharp."

"But Mr. President, I—"

"You have a good job at Right TV. Maybe it pays for a nice place somewhere. It would be a shame for you to lose it overnight. I know many younger girls who would be pleased to have it."

Terror gripped her and she realized what losing her job would mean. She and her daughter would have to move from her Greenwich house back to Virginia. No more accolades, influential meetings with powerbrokers, or genteel Connecticut life. Instead, an existence of obscurity and poverty. And she had no doubt he would make it happen.

"That's better," he said, after she said she would come.

The event took place at the Washington Towers Hotel, a property the president owned. The sleek woman Republican fundraiser at the door crowed to Melody that the average donation was five hundred thousand dollars. The organizers had initially scheduled the dinner for the White House, but watchdog Democrats forced the change of venue.

Inside the large ballroom, as Melody feared, no one wore a mask. Almost all the attendees were men, a few with trophy wives. They coughed and spluttered as they told each other stories of their commercial triumphs. None of them admitted to major problems because of COVID-19.

In the course of the evening, the president challenged the attendees to describe whether the virus had disrupted their business or personal lives. The overwhelming answers were that employees were becoming more of a problem, but that the outbreak had little effect on lifestyle or income of the speaker.

Most of the attendees had decided to move to their country houses. One man groused that his boat mechanic had the nerve to get sick. He did not know how long the man would be out and meanwhile the yacht sat in its mooring useless. "Terrible state of affairs," he complained.

Melody's smile, intelligence, and engaging manner made her a popular conversationalist. As she expected, no social distancing. She continued to feel uncomfortable and could imagine the airborne particles landing on her face as she talked with one self-absorbed tycoon after another.

She also began to analyze more carefully than she had in the past the methods they used to get to their position. Most of them, she decided, had benefited greatly from the generosity of others. Instead of wanting to give back, they were here to figure out how they could maintain the present state of affairs. They were not a noble group of people to be associated with, not a group who thought about others. Especially others beneath them.

By the end of the evening, she felt uncomfortable and used. Not a trophy wife, but a trophy nevertheless.

"See, aren't you glad you came?" the president asked, maskless as always, as Melody and the others exited.

CHAPTER TWENTY-TWO

CORONAVIRUS VISITS MELODY

MARCH 27-APRIL 2, 2020
GREENWICH, CT, AND NEW YORK, NY

Five days after the Washington fundraiser, Melody developed a cough which would not stop despite decongestants. Sore throat and nasal congestion followed. At night she had fevers. She found it hard to take a deep breath and always seemed short of breath.

These symptoms did not stop her from doing her job. She took the commuter rail into the studios three days a week to tape her show. The train was much less crowded than it had been, and she could work as she rode.

This left her with more time to spend with Emily, who now went to school by computer under the supervision of the *au pair.*

Under the new schedule, Melody was home every evening and four days a week. After dinner she and Emily did jigsaw puzzles together, watched movies, and laughed. The *au pair*, who had moved in with them to join the family bubble, had nights and weekends to herself.

The years since she adopted Emily had raced faster than Melody realized. While she had been expanding her television presence and political clout, her growing child had changed from wide-eyed preschooler to sophisticated nine-year-old.

This became evident with discussions over dinner or alone together on leisurely weekends. Sometimes she was ready for the questions:

"Mommy, is climate change bad?

"Why do you ask?"

"My friends at school say it will destroy our generation."

"I don't think there is any good evidence for climate change. Tell your friends there is a cyclicity in weather that they are ignoring. I bet you they won't even know what cyclicity means."

Sometimes the questions were more difficult.

"Why don't I ever see my real mother and father?"

"You know that being adopted means I chose you especially to be with me. Your biological mom and dad are in Colombia. That's very far away, in South America."

"Can I visit them some day?"

"Of course, sweetheart. For now, you and I are the family."

"I'm glad you chose me." Emily snuggled into Melody's side. "I love you, Mommy."

In those days, Melody realized how much her daughter meant to her. It was not just the idea of molding a child's development, though she could see her own traits like stubbornness and demand for excellence take form in her daughter. It was something more basic, a link that overrode every other consideration in her life.

The suspicion that her persistent cough might be more than a cold began to worry her. She believed that the whole coronavirus thing was overplayed, but she wasn't stupid. She knew that God had always protected her, that His plan for her did not include getting sick, but she began to worry about her cough and exhaustion.

One day at the studios, she looked so pale the makeup artist gave up on getting her to her usual tint for the camera. Melody taped her show with as few direct shots as possible. She felt as drained as if she had been up for days.

As she was leaving, she bumped into the network physician. She asked him about her symptoms.

"You definitely need COVID-19 testing," he said.

"No way. You think this stuff about the virus being a serious health concern is real?" she asked.

"You'd have to be deaf and dumb not to believe it. Don't you in your heart know it's a problem?"

"Not really. I think it's just liberal hype."

"It's more than that. I'm a TV personality, but at base I'm a physician, and I believe COVID-19 is a threat. You need to be tested, and I have a couple of test kits in my office. Wait here."

He returned and did the nasal swab standing in the corridor. Her colleagues shot puzzled looks as they scurried by, most of them without masks.

"You'll have to take a couple of days off until we get the results. I can't have one of our staff infecting the whole building and all the guests we see in here."

"No way. I want to work."

"I'm telling you to take a couple of days off."

"You're not my doctor."

"I'm charged with maintaining a healthy workplace."

"But I feel OK, just tired."

"You really don't get it, do you? How you feel is irrelevant. This time off is for the rest of us. If we had enough test kits, I would make a weekly testing mandatory for everyone here, but we can't get them any easier than the rest of the country. This is a matter of thinking about the other people in the world."

It came as no surprise to Melody that her test was positive, but her heart rate increased and she felt faint as the company doctor gave her the results over the phone. An anxiety deep within her bubbled toward the surface. Had she made a lifechanging mistake in minimizing this virus?

"So what do I do? Any medication? Any other treatment?"

"We don't know anything that helps. Take two weeks off work. Do not use hydroxychloroquine. Do use the opportunity to get substantial rest. We'll get another test at the end of two weeks. I have your kit for then already set aside, waiting for your return!"

"What about my daughter?"

"You need to isolate from her until you're clear, try not to get her infected. Can she live with someone else for two weeks?"

"I'll work it out," Melody said, but had no plans to separate herself.

Deep down, she was glad to be ordered not to work. Her

fatigue had become harder and harder to overcome. She also developed new problems: trouble thinking straight, and distorted taste. Food didn't seem right no matter what she ate. She asked the doctor about these symptoms and learned they pointed to COVID-19 as well.

She wasn't sure she could trust the network doctor completely. Seeking another opinion, one that she hoped would be more to her liking, she called Duncan MacGregor.

"Dr. MacGregor, it's Melody Swift. I have a question. A friend of mine has developed COVID-19. Her doctor says she doesn't have to do anything special about her nine-year-old daughter while she's recovering. They can just carry on as usual. I assume that's OK."

"It's nice to hear from you, Ms. Swift. Is your daughter sick?"

"No. This is for a friend."

"Sure. Tell your friend she absolutely must get away from her daughter while she herself recovers. The child may still be free of virus and should be given every chance to remain that way. I assume the daughter has no symptoms."

"Correct."

"Staying together is a recipe for disaster."

"I thought this disease didn't affect children."

"That opinion is changing now. Some children get a delayed but very serious condition related to the coronavirus."

"Thanks."

"Let me know if I can help if anything does happen to your friend's daughter."

Melody stared at the wall. Of course MacGregor knew it was her own daughter, but he didn't push her. She trusted him more than the network doctor, but she still didn't like his recommendations.

She didn't have to do what he or anyone else said. Emily was her child, and she had the final say, not some doctor. She would think about it for a while, then decide how to handle the home situation.

Making a decision about work was easier.

She told her manager she needed two weeks away from the studio and proposed the idea of doing her show from home.

"How do you feel, really?" he asked, staring at her on Zoom.

"A little tired."

"Don't try to fool me. You look completely exhausted. If you did the show looking like you do now, you'd transmit the message that this virus was a big problem no matter what you said. That's not the idea we're supposed to get across. We want to deny this virus, to present it as a minor annoyance or even a hoax."

He looked at the ceiling, a move Melody knew as his response to something he struggled with.

"You're going to have to let someone else do the show."

"Could multiple guests rather than one person host for me?"

"Why? Afraid one replacement might be too good?" he asked with a chuckle. "Melody, you have the third biggest following on the network."

"I know, but I don't want that to change. Maybe Sean and Barker each for a week? They might like the added time slot, and they know the routines. My staff has the topics and guests already set out, so the logistics should be more or less on autopilot. That way my ratings will stay high."

"OK, but don't make this a habit. We need your smiling face back as soon as possible."

For managing her home situation, she decided a modified schedule would be adequate protection. Emily and the *au pair* would work together every day including weekends. Melody would have dinner with her daughter, then spend only one hour with her in the evening. They would even wear masks.

After a week, her respiratory symptoms stabilized to a persistently annoying cough. Her fever resolved. She still felt exhausted and slightly confused. She checked Emily's temperature every day and found no high fever, though Emily had slight temperature elevation and a cough for a few days. Melody lapsed into a kind of limbo state, sleeping more than she ever had, planning future shows, and trying not to think about coronavirus. It was a long two weeks of quarantine.

CHAPTER TWENTY-THREE

"IT'S NO BIG DEAL"

APRIL 16-30, 2020
NEW YORK, NY, AND WASHINGTON, D.C.

At the end of her quarantine period, Melody tried to slip in and out of the Right TV building without being noticed. She had no luck. Colleagues from anchormen to cleaning personnel welcomed her and asked her when she was coming back. Her response was a smile and a shrug. "Depends on the test."

She reported to the doctor's office for the swab.

"I want to get a blood test too," the network doctor said after shoving the long probe to the back of her nose and making her sneeze violently.

"No way. I hate needles. And I can't stand anything to do with blood."

"I need to know you have antibodies to the coronavirus. You're not getting back to work unless I get it."

"This virus business certainly takes away my individual rights, doesn't it?"

"Only if you want to work here," he said without a smile.

"Keeping this place safe is a nightmare. Herding cats is nothing compared to guarding the prima donnas, both male and female, in this building. The men are worse than the women, by the way."

He called her three days later. "I have good news all round," he said. "Your swab was negative, and you have antibodies to COVID-19."

"What does that mean?"

"You've eliminated this particular virus from your respiratory tract, and your body has created protection against it."

Melody sat stunned, then pleased as she considered his comments. She had beaten the coronavirus with only exhaustion and a lot of coughing to show for it.

She decided to use her own experience as the first story when she returned to broadcasting. She began by thanking the men who had taken her show for the two weeks.

"And guess what!" she said. "I was away because I got sick with The Virus, capital T capital V. You know, COVID-19, the so-called scourge of the world. I have antibodies now and so I'm all set for future possible attacks. Living proof that this coronavirus thing can be overcome. It's no big deal."

It was one of the highest-rated segments she had ever done.

She was pleased when the president discussed her situation on his daily coronavirus update the next day. He pointed out that she was an example of a healthy person who got through the virus infection with little problem. "It's no big deal," he said, echoing her final comment on the disease.

When he called her the next day, she thought it would be to expand on those comments. His initial sentence on the call mystified her. "Do you know for certain you have antibodies to the coronavirus in your blood?"

"I do."

"Do you know your blood type?"

"O positive. Why?"

"Great. I want to give you an opportunity to serve your country in a big way."

"Sir?"

"A big opportunity. The biggest of your life, probably."

"How is that?" *Where was this going?*

"My sources tell me the best way to block this virus for now is to use antibodies from someone who's had the infection."

"You mean use the antibodies from another person's blood?"

"Yes."

"You want me to give you my antibodies?"

"Exactly."

"By blood transfusion?"

"Yes. You're a lucky lady. How many Americans get to provide that kind of service to their president? Of course, you can't tell anyone about it. Absolutely no one. Big state secret. The biggest. Protecting your president."

Melody sat stunned.

"But what if I don't—"

"Let me remind you. I am the president. You could lose everything if I just snapped my fingers."

Silence.

He continued. "Be in the medical office at the White House tomorrow at one p.m. Don't be late—I only have an hour."

"But sir, I'm not sure it's a good idea. And is it safe?"

She was talking to a dead phone line.

She did some creative lying to explain why she would miss taping of her show the next morning. One of her subordinates, however, was only too happy to take over on short notice. The guests had already been scheduled, and the process involved less drama than she expected.

At one o'clock the next day, Melody reported to the White House physician's suite. It looked more like an urgent care center than a single doctor's workplace. The guard told her it was a U.S. Navy medical facility, with five offices and a complete emergency room. Normally it served not only the president, vice president, and their families, but also the public touring the White House. With coronavirus, it had been pared down to a small crew.

Today it was empty except for Melody and the nurse-in-charge. "Everyone's at lunch," the nurse explained. She was pure navy, a petite silver-haired woman with a thirty-year service badge beside her name tag. She wore a bright white dress with white shoes and stockings, and a mask. Melody almost expected her to salute.

"Have you given blood before?" the nurse asked.

"Never. I hate everything to do with needles."

"It only hurts for a minute. I'm going to take a unit of your blood, then remove the antibodies and give the rest of the blood back to you."

She tapped a metallic box on a stand beside her. "This little unit cost seventy thousand dollars, but it does everything we need in a few minutes."

"Where is the president?"

"He'll be along at the end. Now can you squeeze the rubber ball a few times for me?"

Melody felt the cold alcohol on her skin, the rubber tourniquet tightening on her arm, the plunge of the needle toward her vein.

"Your vein rolled. I have to do this again," the nurse said and pulled the needle out. She held pressure for a minute, then repeated the puncture in Melody's other arm. This time she seemed satisfied.

After the nurse left, Melody stared at the IV pole beside her, watching her blood drip into the plastic bag, and felt as though she would vomit. Throwing up terrified her even more than giving blood, and she pushed the alarm button.

The nurse appeared immediately, put oxygen prongs into Melody's nose, and patted her on the hand. "That panic button is really meant for emergencies, you know," she said with a tone of reproach.

The cold room, continuing pain in her arm, and knowledge that her blood was dripping slowly out of her body made the half hour that followed one of the most unpleasant in Melody's life. She considered how she had grown up believing that blood was life, and that she had been given no options in being recruited to donate her lifeblood in this way.

Once again in her relationship with the president, she felt used.

The president's arrival a few minutes later improved her spirits a little. He stuck his head into her room, said she was looking good but pale, advised her to put on more makeup before she went back in public, and disappeared.

An hour later the process finished. Melody had hoped she would sleep during part of it, but she could not. The smell of alcohol, bright light glaring into her eyes, and discomfort when she tried to move her arm, kept her wide-eyed and awake.

After the plasma had been returned, the nurse told Melody to rest for a few minutes more to allow the blood loss to equilibrate, then helped her to the door.

"I expect we'll see you in a couple of months again," she said. "These antibody transfusions are only good for about sixty days."

CHAPTER TWENTY-FOUR

GEORGE FLOYD

SUNDAY, MAY 31, 2020
BOSTON, MA

"Would you be willing to do something with me this afternoon?" Lauren asked as she and Mac prepared Sunday brunch. Together they pressed waffles, cut strawberries, and whipped fresh cream for Maggie and Peter to wolf down.

"What's up?" he asked, sensing an uneasy timbre in her voice.

"One of our school parents asked me to join the march against George Floyd's murder."

"I hope you said no?"

"I said I'd talk it over with you. It's important to me, but I'm uncomfortable doing it alone." She nicked her finger with the strawberry knife and ran cold water over it.

Mac dried the finger with a dishtowel. "Why on earth would you expose yourself to the danger of being around all those people?"

"When an unarmed man can be murdered by a police

officer who asphyxiates him, no one is safe. Doesn't matter what the skin color is. I want to show my agreement with the people protesting this killing."

"His murder was wrong, but aren't there other more effective ways you could protest? A crowded demonstration is not a smart place to be. Who asked you to go?"

"Latoya's father," Lauren said.

"I don't want you to go," Mac said as he wrapped a bandage around her finger. "I'm certainly not going. It will be a huge coronavirus spread event. Half the demonstrators won't be wearing masks, and everyone will be shouting and singing and spreading the virus."

"But Mac, how can I say no?"

"Tell Latoya's dad your physician husband said no. Say we had a previous engagement. Say you had an emergency at home. We can watch it all on TV."

Lauren shook her head.

"Remember, too, that you're not just acting for yourself when you make this kind of decision," Mac added. "You have a responsibility not to spread the infection to others, including our children. How would you feel if Maggie got sick?"

"That's a low blow, Mac. They say children don't get COVID-19."

"They're wrong. Some cases have been reported from England of a deadly syndrome in children related to COVID. Attending a big demonstration makes no sense right now."

"OK, I won't go." Lauren said. "I'll tell Latoya's father we can't make it. But I do want to watch it on TV."

"That sounds great. I'd be delighted to join you. I support the cause, but not the march. Not right now."

Melody Swift was not sure she wanted to be at the Floyd demonstration in Boston either. She wasn't worried about coronavirus, because she knew she had antibodies and was immune. It was just that she reserved Sundays to be with her daughter, and the demonstration would cut into that time.

She and Emily didn't see each other much during the week, especially with the coronavirus restrictions she had placed. Now those were over, and the weekend was their time together. Besides, Emily had been feeling mildly unwell for a few days. Nothing specific, but just some stomach pains. Certainly no cough or high fever. Normally Melody would have simply said no to leaving the house.

On the other hand, going to the demonstration was a church obligation. Melody served on the mission and outreach committee of First Babtist Church of Greenwich, which sponsored a Black congregation in the Roxbury section of Boston. She had been asked to attend the Floyd demonstration as the official representative of the Greenwich church.

She asked to be given time off work Monday in case the demonstration went late. Her boss did her one better. He assigned her to go with a videographer Sunday and record the scene, saying that she could take a free day whenever she wanted in the future as payback.

She drove up to Boston Sunday morning. At two o'clock she and her associate met Reverend James Washington at his storefront church in Roxbury, Massachusetts. About fifty congregants, all Black, clustered around him.

The six foot eight Washington looked more like a basketball star than a preacher. He had in fact garnered a great record in college basketball, but had traded the hoop for the pulpit without hesitation when he got the call to ministry. His wire-rimmed spectacles, tailored blue suit, and red silk stole reflected his present role as a religious leader.

"We're blessed to have you with us," Washington said, enveloping Melody's hands in his. "Our congregation is going to join the procession coming up from Nubian Square in a couple of minutes. Will you walk with us?"

They proceeded up Malcom X Boulevard toward Tremont St., listening to the sounds of singing and chattering of voices growing louder. Melody felt uncomfortable as one of the few white faces, but maintained a vigilant demeanor and stuck beside Washington. Her Black cameraman had no trouble.

"We're going to merge with the crowd now," Washington said as their group turned onto Tremont Street, "so stay close."

Melody felt her heart race with anxiety as their group of fifty joined a thousand demonstrators with every skin color from pale white to dark black. The sweet aroma of marijuana hung over some clusters. Police vehicles cleared the street in front of them. Both male and female officers accompanied them on bicycles on either side, often singing with them.

Occasionally someone would break into "Amazing Grace" or "We Shall Overcome," and the crowd would join in tuneful song.

Homemade banners hoisted high.

"*George Floyd*

Breonna Taylor

Michael Ramos
Am I next?

Black Lives Matter

George Floyd, Father, Friend, Son, Mentor
A Human Being

Until the color of your skin is the same as mine you can never understand

No justice, No peace.

I can't breathe

enough is enough

how many more?

Arriving at Boston Common an hour later, Melody stood back as the crowd kneeled on one knee to remember the force that had suffocated the man they were marching for. She didn't want other cameras to catch her participating in the ceremony.

Police officers in the crowd, many of them Black, knelt as well. They held up both arms in a gesture of triumph and joy with the people around them. They shouted "Amen" as the religious leaders in front of the State House preached against racism. Many of the demonstrators wore masks, but just as many did not. Melody, of course, did not. She didn't need them because she was immune, but she didn't want to wear one either.

She had mixed feelings as she watched. She admired the moral strength of the people marching, their willingness to do something that embodied their belief. All her life she had hoped she might someday find that kind of action to give her own life ultimate purpose.

On the other hand, she felt uncomfortable with such a multiracial crowd around her. Her colleagues had instilled in her a fear of people who did not look like her. She wanted to support Reverend Washington and his church, but she really had very little in common with these people.

In any case, she did not think the peaceful demonstration she had participated in thus far would be of interest to her viewers. She did not bother to get any video footage.

As they crossed back to Tremont St, Washington restrained them with an outstretched arm. "Look over there," he said, pointing to a police SUV in front of the Beantown Pub, a block away.

A group of about ten masked demonstrators, all white, did something under the vehicle and then stood back, waving excitedly.

"What's going on?" Melody asked, straining to see.

"Flames behind the car," Washington said.

"Get this," Melody shouted at her cameraman. In a moment, a fiery halo engulfed the car. Several young men in the crowd cheered and took selfies silhouetted by the blazing police cruiser.

Washington shook his head and moved swiftly across Tremont Street at a pace Melody could barely match. She left her cameraman taking videos.

"What's going on?" she shouted.

"False flags," Washington replied.

"False flags?"

"Agitators pretending to be with us but here to cause violence. They hijack a demonstration and use it to loot and burn. I must let the police supervisor know what's coming down."

At the corner, a white man with shaved head and tattoos on his neck lifted his skateboard and shattered a portion of storefront window. A dozen Black men ringed the storefront to prevent further breakage, yelling, "What are you doing? This is not what we came for."

"That's what you think," the skinhead said, lifting his arm again.

Washington twisted the agitators's arm as he swung it back. The man yelped in pain and dropped the board.

"Get out of here," Washington shouted. "Now." He continued his march. Melody's cameraman joined her again, running to keep up as they worked their way toward a cluster of police vehicles blocking lower Washington Street. The pedestrian region was now packed, with the shouts of demonstrators, the smell of alcohol and marijuana, and the grit of street dirt swirled by too many feet.

Washington found a police official and spoke for several minutes, then returned to Melody and those around her.

"I tried to convince him to be aggressive against these interlopers who have taken over our peaceful demonstration.

I've seen these hooligans at work before. Violence is their main goal, and if they can make a little extra money by breaking shop windows and stealing stuff, so much the better. Let's get out of here. It may not be safe now. We can get on the Orange Line just up the street."

He led them toward the subway when a pickup truck raced toward them. Washington jumped in its way to make it stop.

It didn't.

It hit him at the hip, knocking him to the side of the road. Melody could see the thug who Washington had interfered with hunched over the steering wheel. The man grinned, gave her the finger, and reversed the car, screeching with smoking tires back onto the street and out of sight.

Melody ran over to Washington, who lay crumpled and groaning on the ground. A cluster of police officers raced toward them, one calling an ambulance as they came. The videographer caught the image of Washington squirming in pain.

The EMTs arrived within a minute. Reverend Washington disappeared into the back of the van.

"I got what I came for!" Melody cried exultantly. Her boss, viewers, and the president would be pleased to have proof that the event was violent. She knew the violence was a deliberate intrusion by white agitators. That was a mere inconvenience to a great story about demonstrators turning violent and the danger to law-abiding citizens. Her trip to Boston had been worth the trouble after all.

She returned to Greenwich pleased with herself, getting home before midnight. She checked on Emily, who seemed warm when she gave her a kiss but otherwise appeared to be sleeping normally. She didn't ask her how her belly was feeling.

CHAPTER TWENTY-FIVE

CHILDREN'S WARD

MONDAY, JUNE 1, 2020
BOSTON, MA

Except for the call about her hypothetical friend, Mac did not hear from Melody at all in April and May. The coronavirus took its toll in Massachusetts in that time, and many of the restrictions he had seen in Wuhan were implemented. The governors of the New England states worked along with the New York governor to develop scientific guidelines for management of the pandemic.

All retail stores and restaurants were shuttered, except grocery, pharmacy, and other essential outlets. Schools, universities, and offices closed and those who still had jobs worked from home. There were no sports events, concerts, or other social gatherings of any kind. All parks, swimming pools, and playgrounds were locked.

Hospitals filled up with COVID-19 patients, but the preparations made collaboratively months before allowed them to handle the onslaught without the terrible conditions of the Bronx. The death toll continued at hundreds a week, especially in the elderly, Hispanic, and Black populations.

Social distancing and wearing of masks were mandatory in most Massachusetts towns. Subway and bus lines continued but at markedly reduced levels. Nationally, airplane travel was curtailed.

Despite the evidence that the case load in the United States was increasing, the White House advocated the removal of social distancing restrictions with the claim that the virus was going away.

At five a.m. on the first day of June, Mac's cell phone jangled him awake.

"Duncan MacGregor here."

"Mac, it's Melody Swift."

Mac knew her voice. More important, he knew that distinctive tone. He had heard it hundreds of times in desperate patients, could almost feel the fear that drove it. "You OK?"

"Not me. Emily."

"Emily?"

"My nine-year old."

"What happened?" Mac moved out of the bedroom to avoid waking Lauren.

"She had a slight stomach ache two days ago. I thought it was the flu, or maybe a reaction to the fact that I had to go away yesterday. A few minutes ago, she woke me up because her hands and feet were sore. They're all red, and she also has a rash on her arms. I'm worried she might have Mono or Lyme disease."

"She needs a doctor right away."

"I fired my pediatrician six months ago."

"Then take her to the hospital."

"I don't trust any of the hospitals here. I know I can trust you because of the way you treated my sister. I want to bring her to you."

"I'm not sure she's safe to travel."

"She's fine except for the rash and fever. I can have a private plane ready at Westchester County Airport in half an hour and be at Logan an hour after that."

"But—"

"I'm not asking you, Mac, I'm telling you. Can you meet me at the hospital?"

"Of course. I'll meet the plane if you come, but—"

"*When* I come, not *if*. I'll arrive at Logan at seven a.m. I have to get going."

Mac stood with the phone in his hand for a few seconds. From the description, this sounded like the newly reported syndrome that can follow COVID-19 infection in children.

He hoped that he was wrong, that Melody's daughter was not the hypothetical child Melody had called him about. He prayed she did not have the devastating disorder starting to be diagnosed around the world.

In his heart, he believed that was exactly what she had, and felt both anger and despair. Children should not have to suffer because the adults around them deny a disease's seriousness.

He put into action the steps necessary to get Emily pre-admitted in case she was too sick to go through the usual process: called Denise Miller, the director of the hospital's pediatric ICU, to reserve a bed, informed the night admitting office that he would get insurance information to them later in the day if Melody could not provide it at check-in, and notified the administrator on call responsible for COVID-19 admissions.

He left a voice mail on his own clinic administrator's phone, relieved he did not have to talk to her directly about cancelling his morning clinic. He shook his head as he imagined her explaining to hospital administration and patients that he would be late or even absent.

He shaved and dressed and was in his car on Storrow Drive by six-thirty. Waiting a few seconds to enter the Callahan tunnel, he remembered the long line that he would have endured three months before.

He followed the inner Logan roads to the private air terminal, spotting Melody before she saw him. A thin pale child slumped in the wheelchair beside her.

"Thank God you're here even though we arrived early," Melody said. "I had to ask for help in deplaning. Emily seems totally exhausted."

Mac evaluated the child quickly. She was listless, dry, and floppy. She didn't open her eyes when spoken to. A spotty rash covered her arms. Her palms were red, and skin flaked from them in some places. The whites of her eyes were red. When he felt the enlarged lymph nodes in her neck, he realized she also had a significant fever. He pulled down on her jaw to look at her tongue. It was twice as large as normal and cherry red.

Melody gasped. "Her tongue was not like that when

we left."

"I'm surprised they let you on the plane, even though it was a private jet."

"The attendant was a fan of mine. Watches *Swift Currents* regularly."

"We need to move," Mac said as he grabbed the wheelchair and pushed it toward the car as fast as safety would allow.

Melody panted to keep up, rolling the bags behind her. "Do you know what this is?"

"Yes, I believe I do."

"Is it Lyme?"

"I don't think so, but I'd prefer to have confirmation before we talk about it." Now at the car, he moved Emily into the back seat and adjusted the seat belt so she could lie down.

"If she's admitted, I've got gold-plate insurance. I want the best. That's why I came to you."

Mac said nothing but helped her into the car and drove as quickly as he could toward the hospital. Traffic had increased, and he tapped the wheel impatiently. "The ride should only be seven minutes, but it might be a little longer today," he said.

She twisted her hands and looked out the window.

"It's not your fault," he said as gently as he could.

"She was fine three days ago. I don't understand."

"There are some questions I have to ask, and the other doctors will ask too. I believe you had coronavirus since I last saw you?"

Tears welled in Melody's eyes as she nodded. "A month

ago."

"Did you get tested?"

"Yes, at work."

"I thought you didn't believe in tests," Mac said, remembering that the president had recently discouraged testing because it made America's numbers look bad.

"If it means keeping my job, I'll get tested."

"How bad was the infection for you?"

"I had a different experience than you did. Just a fever, cough and sore throat with a chest pain. Some confusion and loss of smell. Exhaustion the main problem, still not gone. And I still have trouble keeping my thoughts straight. The whole thing lasted two weeks. Too bad you don't watch my show. I did a segment on it. Really not a big deal."

Mac's frustration broke through his attempt to remain civil. "Is *really not a big deal* some kind of new buzzword for denying COVID-19? I heard the president use exactly those words."

"I said that on my show. For me, it was just like a bad flu."

"I can tell you it was a really big deal for me and for thousands of people like me. For my father-in-law and over a hundred thousand people like him, it was fatal."

She looked away, tears remaining in the corner of her eyes. Mac could swear she was remembering something. He resumed his gentler tone. "Anything else about your experience?"

"No."

"Has Emily been at home all the time?"

"Yes. Some of the day she has an *au pair* with her."

"Did you get her tested after you got sick?"

"Of course not. She wasn't sick. She hasn't had severe cough or congestion or even a sore throat. Are we here?"

They approached the curving entrance to the hospital, where dozens of people lined up six feet apart, all masked.

She turned to Mac with a look of horror.

"Do we have to wait in that line?"

"No, that's for grownups. We're entering there." He drove to a brightly painted door marked *Children's Emergency.*

Emily, curled up in the back seat, shook vigorously as they arrived. Mac lifted her as tenderly as he would have carried his own daughter Maggie. He nodded at the check-in clerk, calling Emily's name over his shoulder as they rushed into the pediatric treatment area.

"Is the hospital still in business?" Melody asked as she looked around the empty space. "There's no one here."

"People are afraid to come in because of COVID-19."

A Black woman with mask, shield, gloves, gown, and shoe covers entered their cubicle.

"Are you our nurse?" Melody asked.

"This is Dr. Miller, the head of our pediatric intensive care unit," Mac said. "Denise, this is Ms. Swift."

"Yes, I know Ms. Swift from Right TV," Miller replied. "Not too fond of doctors or any other so-called "experts," as I remember."

Mac continued without giving Melody a chance to speak. "Melody's nine-year old daughter Emily started with arthralgias and an exanthem three days ago. Today she has palmar erythema and some desquamation as well as lymphadenopathy."

Dr. Miller looked at the thermometer reading, palpated for a pulse, read the sphygmomanometer, and said, "Mac, please take Ms. Swift to the waiting area."

Melody stood. "This is my daughter. I'm staying here."

"Now, please. Emily has a very low blood pressure. She's going into shock." She began to prepare the left shoulder area with Betadine.

"What's she doing?" Melody asked Mac.

"We need a central line," Miller said.

"An intravenous? You can't do this without my consent. Don't you know who I am? I'll sue you and destroy the hospital's reputation." Deep inside, something asked her why she would lash out like that, but the need to protect her daughter kept her defiant.

Dr. Miller paused. "Ma'am, your daughter could die in the next few minutes if we don't get her fluids and medication. I know you think doctors are a bunch of quacks, but this quack is going to do everything she can to keep Emily alive. Walking through that door gives implicit consent for treatment, and Mac will explain what we need to do. Won't you, Mac?" She turned back to the skin preparation with antiseptic.

"Come with me," Mac said, using a tone that broached no discussion. As they exited, they heard a code blue call to the pediatric emergency room go out over the hospital p.a. system.

BURIAL OF THE DEAD

CHAPTER TWENTY-SIX

INTENSIVE CARE

MONDAY, JUNE 1, 2020
BOSTON, MA

Melody pulled away as Mac guided her to the exit. "I don't need help," she said, feeling frightened and betrayed. She had not anticipated that doctors would puncture her child with an enormous needle and not let her stay to comfort her. She wished there were someone she could blame there and then.

"You have to trust us," Mac said as they took seats in the family conference room, a comfortable space with thick blue carpet and armchairs positioned six feet apart. The music of Mozart added a gentle tone. Canvas prints of Provence and Greece graced the walls.

Although she initially felt the urge to scream, "Why should I?", the tranquil room and Mac's worried expression above his mask led her to reply, "I never trust anyone. But I'll go along with you. For now."

"We're doing the best we can."

"I'll never forgive you if she dies. You have no idea how precious she is to me."

"We can deal with this condition, but it does take a team. And sometimes we must move fast to prevent disaster. That's what you just saw."

"You say 'this condition' as if you know what she has."

"I don't want be wrong. We'll have the answer for sure by tomorrow morning."

"About that 'we'. I came to *you* for help, not some woman doctor I've never met."

"Melody, you may not understand how a hospital like this works. Each person here has a special expertise, which we use to make the whole better than any individual. That's why we're ranked number one in the country, and that's why I rely on the expertise of others for things I don't know."

"Isn't that just a copout to avoid taking responsibility for your own decisions?" She felt herself moving beyond all filters of gentility. She had to fight someone at this moment, and in a paradoxical way she considered Mac a safe opponent.

"No, actually not." Mac spoke gently, as if he understood what she was doing, without anger but with a firm tone. "Asking for help is just admitting that someone knows more than I do. Anyway, why don't you check into your hotel and come back at one?"

"Just don't tell me it's COVID-19. Emily had no cough or trouble breathing, just fever and rash. I'll be furious if you try to pass it off as coming from that fake coronavirus."

"Let's wait for the lab results."

Melody could not leave the hospital despite Mac's suggestion to go to the hotel. She stood in the bathroom for five minutes, then returned to the waiting room after he left. When a solicitous nurse told her that visitors could not wait in the hospital waiting rooms, she moved down the hall to another waiting room.

After half an hour there, with the same result, she relocated to a waterfront bench behind the hospital, near enough to the pediatric ward to be in spiritual touch. She had the feeling that if she stayed close, her will would combine with Emily's to achieve success.

She paced back and forth, checking her watch every few minutes. She cursed her powerlessness. She had spent her life treating every obstacle as a ladder rung and pulling herself up on it. It now felt now as if the ladder was falling on top of her.

At ten to one, she returned to the waiting room. Mac appeared with Dr. Miller right at one. Miller described what they had done, explaining that Emily had stabilized but still required close monitoring. Her kidney function was compromised, she showed some evidence of abnormal blood clotting, and her heartbeat was irregular at times.

"I want to stay in the ICU with my daughter," Melody said.

"We can't allow that," Miller said. "It's against hospital policy because it's too great a risk to you, our hospital personnel, and other patients."

"I want to know you're not hurting my daughter, not experimenting with her."

"I'm sorry. This is an absolute hospital rule."

Melody's pulse accelerated as her anger rose. Her cheeks

heated. For this woman to tell her she couldn't see her daughter—

"I need to talk to your department head," she barked.

"I *am* the department head," Miller replied.

"Who do you report to?"

"The president of the hospital."

"Then get me him."

"You mean her. Her name is Susan Renwick. You can reach her office through the central hospital number."

"I want to see her now."

Miller shrugged. "I don't keep her appointment book. You'll have to arrange that on your own."

Melody looked at Mac expectantly.

"I don't run Dr. Renwick's schedule either," he said, also shrugging.

"Great patient service," Melody said, trying to layer her voice with sarcasm. The mask diluted the effect. "I'll take this up when I return to the hotel. Can I at least see my daughter now?"

"No."

Melody stamped her foot, feeling like a five-year-old. She couldn't help it. She had not been so frustrated for a long time. "You mean after flying all the way up here and hearing a code blue called on my daughter, I can't even see her? How do I know she's doing better? She could be dead."

Miller's frown was evident even behind her mask. She punched numbers into her cell, asked the person who answered to show Emily to her mother, and displayed the screen to Melody. Melody tried to grab the phone from

Miller, but was unsuccessful. "She's still very drowsy," Miller said, "but you can see she's stable. We haven't had to intubate her yet."

"Yet? Are you kidding? No way you're going to put a tube in her throat," Melody said. She shouted at the phone, "Emily, Emily, it's mummy." No response from the child, who looked comfortably asleep.

"You can talk to her every day by FaceTime," Mac said. "I know it's hard, but it's better than nothing."

"When do I hear the diagnosis?"

"We should have the data back tomorrow about ten," Mac said. "I suggest a Zoom call with you, me, Dr. Miller, and Emily's nurse."

Miller nodded agreement. "I have to get back to the unit now. Our interactions will be electronic for the next few days." She seemed eager to get out of Melody's presence.

"I know this is hard," Mac said. "I can assure you that Emily is in the best possible hands. To tell the truth, I'm more worried about you than I am about her right now. Will you be OK alone?"

"Of course. That's when I do best."

After Mac left, Melody sat a few minutes to jot some comments in her notebook. She would keep a list of policies and events she found distasteful. Someday they might make a great story to condemn this place.

CHAPTER TWENTY-SEVEN

WAITING

MONDAY, JUNE 1, 2020
BOSTON, MA

Melody checked into the hotel frustrated about her access to Emily and fearful about her daughter's future. The front desk clerk welcomed her and noted that the facility had just reopened.

She paid no attention. This episode in her life was not going as planned. What kind of distorted health care system kept a mother away from her child? How could a virus invade the holiest of sanctuaries, the family?

She called Dr. Renwick's office, demanding an appointment right away. The secretary pointed out that all hospital administrative personnel were working from home, but that he would leave a message for his boss.

Dr. Renwick called an hour later. Sympathetic, she also seemed implacable. When Melody threatened to have her removed, she did not quake. "Our rules are made for your safety as well as for others. I hope you will understand. I wish your daughter well. If you need to speak with someone, we have counsellors available any time. Thank you for your concern." She severed the connection before Melody could unload.

Bitch, Melody wrote in her notebook.

She realized she had not made any arrangement for future episodes of *Swift Currents*, although she had already taped tonight's episode. She called her manager.

"Jim, it's Melody."

"Do you think I could mistake that sweet voice for anyone else? What's up?"

"I need to take a couple of weeks off again. My daughter's sick."

Jim's voice hardened. "Do you mean two weeks, or is that just a guess? This isn't a grocery store, where we just dole out sick days whenever you need them. How long exactly will you be gone?"

"I don't know."

He paused for several seconds. She thought perhaps the line had disconnected, but the timer on the phone kept running. "OK. I'm going to have to let Brianna stand in for you. I can't ask our boys to cover again."

"Whatever. I'm available on cell if whoever you pick has questions, but my staff has the guest list and knows my approach. I'm sure she'll do a great job."

"Melody?"

"Yes."

"I'm really sorry you have to go through all this. First you, then your daughter. This coronavirus thing may be a big deal after all. I'll do my best to keep the wolves from the door. Please take care of yourself."

"Thank you. It's awful, Jimmy. And you're the only person besides Duncan MacGregor who seems to give a damn."

For the rest of the afternoon, she explored the waterfront. The sun shone brilliantly with seventy-five-degree heat and the breeze softly carried the smell of sea air.

She loved Boston harbor. The Hudson river development in New York had open vistas as well, but there was something about looking across the Atlantic Ocean from Boston that thrilled her. For her, this city provided a perfect mix of seaport and sophistication.

She could see big differences in activity compared with March as she wandered. Long Wharf now had more ferries coming and going. Several restaurants on the water prepared patios for outdoor dining. A few children cavorted on the Rose Kennedy freeway or splashed under the fountain, although the carousel was still silent.

On Congress Street, the Convention Center had been converted to a field hospital called Boston Hope for 1000 overflow COVID-19 patients, including the homeless. Vans came and went with regularity, and volunteer health care workers helped patients in and out of the huge entrance. Here was a community coronavirus response at its best. The usual lines of traffic had returned to the area to enter freeways going north, west, or south.

Somewhere in the depths of her brain, doubt began to grow about her position on coronavirus. She had really believed COVID-19 was an atypical flu, a Democratic ploy, or a minor annoyance. In her day-to-day life, she had not seen its real effects. Her colleagues and support staff worked at Right TV as usual, ignoring any coronavirus threat.

Were New Englanders inappropriately compulsive? Or did they grasp something she and her coworkers were missing in their daily reports? She watched a few minutes of the Right TV late show, but found herself strangely uneasy about the cheery content and deliberate avoidance of what she now perceived as the truth about COVID-19.

It was real, and it was incredibly dangerous.

CHAPTER TWENTY-EIGHT

WORSENING

TUESDAY, JUNE 2, 2020
BOSTON, MA

When she logged into next morning's Zoom meeting, Melody gasped at the image of Emily, motionless in bed, eyes closed, body crisscrossed by oxygen tubes, monitor leads, and intravenous lines. A dressing over her collar bone hid the large IV catheter Dr. Miller had inserted in the emergency room.

She longed to take her daughter into her arms and hug her, feel the silky hair cascading over her shoulders, smell the fresh soap of her skin, hear her soft voice.

Dr. Miller began. "Emily's blood pressure has improved but she still requires intensive care. We have the data we need to make a diagnosis. She has a newly-described disease of children called Multisystem Inflammatory Syndrome."

"What causes it?" Melody asked, dreading the answer she already guessed from recent news reports.

"COVID-19 infection. It typically occurs a few weeks after the actual infection. The syndrome is thought to be a delayed immune reaction to the coronavirus. It only occurs in children. There's a similar condition well known to us called Kawasaki disease which—"

Melody interrupted. "I don't want to hear any more right now."

"But I have to ask some questions about therapy."

"Can I call you back? I need a few minutes." Melody pressed the *leave meeting* icon and watched the images fade.

She sat staring at the dark computer screen for several minutes, seeing in it the faces of fellow Right TV announcers who had made light of COVID-19. She saw Republican leaders, none wearing a mask, reassuring the world that the virus was nothing, that no precautions would be needed. She saw the president repeating her own phrases.

"It's just a hoax perpetrated by Democrats."

"It's no worse than the flu. Maybe it is the flu."

"It's not bad—maybe one percent get sick."

What if that one percent includes the person you love most in the world?

She had not considered the possibility that someone close to her would get sick with this virus, let alone die. She had always believed she was one of the chosen, that God would protect her and those she loved from harm. If she did the right thing, her heavenly Father would assure a good life. Being really ill with Covid-19 was not in the deal.

The idea that she had probably infected her own daughter, might have permanently hurt her, and that Emily was by no means safe yet. . .

She bit her upper lip as her eyes filled with tears.

Her screen buzzed with an invitation, *Dr. Duncan*

MacGregor. She wiped her eyes, adjusted her jersey, and clicked the *join meeting* icon.

Mac frowned from the screen.

"You OK?" he asked.

"How can you be so sure about this diagnosis?" she shouted at the screen, releasing the frustration and anger building within her. "I don't believe it. Can you absolutely prove to me that this is caused by the coronavirus?"

"I can understand your anger," Mac said. "Let's go through the data. First, by your own account she was exposed a few weeks ago when you were sick."

Melody interjected. "But she also had exposure to the *au pair.* It may not have been me."

"Of course," Mac said. "I'm just suggesting that there was at least one exposure we know of."

"Second, her skin rash, mouth sores, red eyes, and fever are typical for this disease."

"But can't they also be part of Lyme disease? It can produce a rash."

"It doesn't give mouth sores, red tongue, or reddened eyes. Third, she has coronavirus in her nose and blood."

Melody remained silent.

"Fourth, her markers for inflammation are abnormal. Her sedimentation rate is elevated at 80, C-reactive protein greater than five. Too few lymphocytes and too many neutrophils. I can explain more if you wish, but her body is showing a huge immune response."

"And you can guarantee me only COVID-19 will elevate all these?"

"No. Other infections and immune diseases may as well."

"Mono?"

"Doesn't give this pattern."

"But there are lots of inflammations that affect the body. Couldn't it be from one of those?" Listening to herself, Melody realized how desperate she had become to deny what she knew was true, and to block the guilt that came with it.

"Again, it's the combination that makes the diagnosis. Fifth, she has breakdown of at least five body systems. Her heart shows a low ejection fraction and her serum brain natriuretic peptide is too high. Both of these findings suggest heart failure. Her kidneys are not working either. She has muscle protein in her blood, meaning that she is destroying her own muscle tissue. Her platelets are low. And she has a chest X-ray which looks like early pneumonia."

Melody remained silent now, shaking her head.

Mac continued. "Finally, number six. When she got here, she was going into what we call toxic shock. COVID-19 is one of the few inflammatory diseases that can produce that. Her shock is improving now, but she still requires intensive treatment."

Melody had put her head in her hands during the recitation and looked up with tears in her eyes. "So no question this is COVID-19 related?"

"It fulfills all CDC guidelines for diagnosing this new disease."

"What was the treatment choice Dr. Miller was talking about?"

"We want to give Emily immunoglobulin intravenously, but we thought you should know about the risks."

"What's immunoglobulin?"

"A mixture of antibodies that might attack the virus."

Melody thought back to the president's demand for her antibodies. "Are they specific?"

"No, and that's part of the issue. There is a small possibility of an allergic reaction to the donor's proteins. It's rare."

"Could I give my own antibodies to her?"

"We don't have a protocol for doing that, and the transfusion might add something we don't want to her blood stream. My recommendation is just to go with the immunoglobulin."

"Whatever you want. I'll sign anything. Just keep my daughter alive."

CHAPTER TWENTY-NINE

PROGRESS

JUNE 3-19, 2020
BOSTON, MA

At the next morning's Zoom conference call, Melody was informed that her daughter had not worsened and was holding her own. The doctors said a lack of deterioration could be viewed as a positive sign. Perhaps in a day or two they could hope for improvement.

Dr. Miller signed off, leaving only Mac on the call.

"Melody, I'm so sorry you have to go through this," Mac said. "It would be hard enough if you could spend every minute with Emily. Being apart like this must be terrible."

"I love her more than I would if she were my biological daughter."

"How long have you two been together?"

"Eight years. I adopted Emily in Colombia when she was one. I thank my God every day for her. I think I'd die if she left me now."

The next week blurred for Melody. She would wake up exhausted and fretful, FaceTime the ICU nurse at about nine a.m. for the report, and hear what was planned for the rest of the day. The nurse would usually transmit a view of the hospital cubicle.

The scene did not change. A pale child lying motionless, hair splayed, eyes closed. Intravenous lines, nasal oxygen, and monitor leads for electrocardiogram and blood oxygen level. Arterial catheter for blood pressure.

Some mornings Melody cried, and some she didn't. As she drank the coffee she had just brewed in the room, she watched her Right TV colleagues on the morning show. It was the same message over and over. COVID-19 was a hoax, not a big problem. The president was doing a great job managing the outbreak. The CDC, doctors, and the World Health Organization were all doing a terrible job. Democrats were using this so-called pandemic to keep the president from being re-elected.

The room became stagnant despite the daily cleaning. Clothes piled up on the chairs and dresser tops.

Within a few days she tired of the saccharine smiles and misapplied energies of the co-workers she once imitated. She found their message repugnant now. *Wasn't her daughter living proof that this virus was a serious threat*?

To escape, she would trek to the waterfront and watch life return slowly to what she had once considered the most active area of Boston. The cruise ship *Odyssey* remained moored day and night outside her hotel. Water taxis picked up and discharged occasional passengers. In the harbor, selected ferries resumed their routes. At Logan Airport, a small number of airplanes arrived or departed.

On many days, the goal of her mini-expedition was the Shrine of Our Lady of Good Voyage on Seaport Boulevard. Although it was Roman Catholic rather than evangelical protestant in its tradition, it drew her in through the silence of the sanctuary and the beauty of the stained glass windows.

In this place she began to question her God.

When she was fourteen, she had come to Jesus in a blaze of light while she meditated on a picture of him suffering on the cross. The conviction of her own salvation and of Jesus' presence in her life had remained ever since.

Now she realized a large part of her religion had been more social than spiritual. Growing up, she had the comfort of her evangelical megachurch, the reassuring social message that God would take care of everything in this life or the next. The affluent lifestyle she and her fellow congregants enjoyed proved that He was taking care of them even then.

Like her parents before her, she contributed money, was encouraged by the pastor to be a church leader, and thoroughly enjoyed the combination of local prestige and good deeds that came from regular church going and giving.

When she left for Greenwich, she continued to send money to the church. Neither her sister's fatal brain tumor nor her parents' death in the car accident shook her faith. She firmly believed it was all part of God's plan.

In the chapel, the aura was different. Instead of the social energy of a prosperous congregation, she sensed the collective anguish of thousands of individual despairing souls.

These souls had prayed for fair winds and gotten foul storms, had lost brothers and sisters and sons to the sea, had suffered agony as part of their everyday life. She was at once fascinated and repelled by what she felt there. Prayers that once rolled off her lips now stuck in her throat.

She usually left the chapel feeling more depressed than when she entered. Yet she returned.

In the initial week away from work, she spoke regularly to her news staff. At first, they exclaimed how much they missed her and urged her to hurry back. After a few days, the conversation was about how interesting they found working with her temporary replacement.

She called her producer every afternoon for the first week.

"So when are you coming back?" Jimmy would ask.

"Don't know yet."

"A ballpark figure?"

"No idea. I would have said if I knew."

"Your stand-in is doing a good job. Maybe too good."

In the past she would have said nothing about this implicit threat but would have agonized about it in private. Now she challenged him.

"Are you suggesting that I'm going to be fired?" she asked.

"Of course not. Nothing like that. I miss you and need you. Really, your broadcasts are incisive and provocative. No comparison with your temporary replacement. Not even close."

She didn't much care about his response either way.

There were other ways she was changing as well. In the past, she would have been continuously angry because she could not see her daughter. Now she realized there were other people who could be infected, that the disease could be spread by anyone, that even she could become a super-spreader now that she had been infected once.

She began to trust the people taking care of Emily, who seemed both caring and professional.

Most of all she came to trust Mac more and more. He met with her via Zoom at four o'clock every day and answered every question, responded to every angry defensive comment. He always ended with something like, "We're hopeful she will continue to improve tomorrow."

A few days after arriving, she flew into a panic after Mac told her ECMO was going to be necessary.

"What's ECMO?"

"Extra-corporeal membrane oxygenation. It's a way of providing a temporary artificial heart and lungs."

"Like cardiac bypass?"

"Yes, but for several days. Until the body can take over on its own."

She called her friends back in New York, who had never heard of ECMO. She talked to the Right TV physician and the medical reporter for CNN she had known since her time there. They each described ECMO with great patience and said it was lifesaving, essentially repeating what Mac had said.

She consented, but found the stress of handing her daughter's minute-to-minute life support over to strangers almost intolerable. Her heart felt as if it were caked in ice. She stopped putting on makeup, did her Zoom calls with her photograph on the screen, and let her hair fall where it may.

Every morning she stared at the transmitted image of her daughter in a drug-induced coma with a large machine beside her. Tubing stretched from Emily to the machine, circled, and returned to the thin body. In the process, Emily's blood was being filtered and reoxygenated. Was her soul being drained as well? The knowledge that that machine was the only thing that stood between Emily and death became increasingly impossible to deal with.

Time began to unravel. She fell asleep in the middle of the day, ate from the room service menu or just had coffee, and stopped going out of the hotel. She no longer bothered to watch Right TV or any other channel. News outside the hospital did not interest her.

Ten days after she arrived, she stared at herself in the mirror—thin face, eyes hollowed by fear and grief, blond hair in rat's nests. She smelled of sweat left over from her nocturnal tossing. She wore a nightgown most of the day and rarely brushed her teeth. She decided she looked and felt like a homeless person.

Her soul was as badly deranged as her body. She prayed incessantly, made bargains with God to trade her life for Emily's, berated God for letting her down. She identified with the biblical character Job. He said, "I know that my Redeemer lives." She was not convinced that any redeemer lived to save her daughter.

Perhaps, she thought, she was more like Job's wife, who suggested the best response to this situation was to curse God and die.

She asked to see the counsellor the hospital president had suggested. The therapist, a woman in her fifties, seemed kind and understanding even on a Zoom channel. Melody answered her questions patiently.

Yes, she knew this was probably the best hospital in the country.

Yes, she knew young people were resilient.

Yes, she knew that new treatments were constantly being discovered

Yes, she had faith in the doctors.

After completing the third Zoom therapy session, she sat screaming at the wall.

A knock at the door stopped her.

"Ms. Swift, is everything OK?"

"Yes, sorry. I left the TV on too loud."

"Let us know if we can help in any way."

On the fourteenth day, Mac smiled as he began his session.

"Good news," he said. "Emily seems to have turned a corner. Her blood oxygen levels are rising, and her chest is clearing. "

"You think she's getting better?"

"Absolutely, and other systems are also improving."

Melody hardly knew what to do with this information. Could she trust it? Did it really mean anything?

Two days later, the intensivists took Emily off ECMO and lightened sedation so she could move around in bed.

Which she started to do. Day by day, Melody saw her daughter emerge from her COVID-19 slumber. More movement. Oxygen requirement lessening. Blood chemistries and cell counts returning toward normal.

Mac and the doctors directly involved in her care reported that the immune hyperactivity was diminishing and her heart, kidneys, brain, and lungs were recovering.

The nurses displayed every step in the daily report, proudly itemizing her progress. Melody watched as her daughter sat up in bed for the first time, spoke to her, took the first steps. It was like a bizarre reality TV show.

But it was interactive, and Melody decided she did not want to appear distressed or unkempt. She began showering and combing her hair and putting on makeup again. Food still had no appeal and her muscles were weak simply from lack of exercise, but she started walking by the harbor again and occasionally munched on a lobster roll.

Shortly after that, Mac informed Melody that Emily could be released. "But we think it best she go to a rehab."

"No way," Melody said. "I'm taking her home. We can arrange all the physiotherapy we want there."

"There are still problems that can occur, and she will need a complex set of medications."

"No discussion. I can take care of it. Just tell me what time I should be there."

She began to feel like her old self, itching to arrange things. The *au pair* had quit during the hospitalization. Despite that and Mac's insistence on rehab, Melody proclaimed her daughter would be best treated at home.

Nineteen days and three hours after she had brought her daughter to the hospital, Melody carried Emily into a limousine bound for her home.

CHAPTER THIRTY

RECOVERY

JUNE 19-23, 2020
GREENWICH, CT

Back in Greenwich, Melody woke early the next morning to check on her daughter. Sunlight poured through the window, dappled by the maple tree in the back yard. No sound except Emily's raspy breathing broke the morning silence. Lavender freshener filled the air with its fragrance.

Melody sat on the edge of Emily's bed, stroking her daughter's hair and thinking back on the adventure of adoption. Decision, travel, waiting, first meeting. In the eight years since Emily had joined her, so much had happened. She felt that somehow Emily had reassembled fragments taken from her into a delightful, amazing nine-year-old person.

Emily stirred, opened her eyes.

"Good morning, princess. Want some breakfast?"

Head shake no.

"I have Unicorn cereal. Got it as a special treat."

Emily opened her eyes again, but just stared at the ceiling.

"Ice cream? I can make an exception to our usual rules because it's so great to be home with you."

Same listless headshake.

"What would you like to do today?"

Her daughter sank back onto the pillow.

"How about a YouTube cartoon?"

No change.

"Emily, you can't just lie there. You have to do something. Let's go for a walk around the yard. We can get a little exercise."

Helped by her mother, Emily swung out of bed, walked a few paces around the room, and headed back to bed.

Melody found the first days back in Greenwich harder than the hospitalization. Although her home was beautiful, it had never been a focus of her life. She had not taken time to speak with her neighbors or spend time with them in any activities. She felt more connected to Mac and Boston than to her own neighborhood.

She also felt uncertain about what she should be doing and what normal recovery should look like. She tried to reconnect with her pediatrician's group, but when they remembered that she had fired them, they were not available. She tried three other pediatric offices and found them all suddenly closed to new patients after she told her story of Emily's COVID infection.

Melody tried to pray, but the image of her fragile nine-year-old intruded on any conversations with the God she had left. In her darkest moments, she wondered if Satan had stolen the soul of her child.

Melody made a Zoom appointment with the pastoral care minister at her church, the woman who was charged with hospital visitations and funerals.

"Just remember, God doesn't give you more than you can handle," the middle-aged minister said with a voice oozing sympathy after she heard the story.

"He must think I'm a lot stronger than I am," Melody answered with bitterness in her heart and voice. "I'm past the breaking point."

"His ways are beyond our comprehension. I'm sure some day after this agonizing experience you will find out why this happened to you." Melody saw the pastor take a quick look at the clock and accepted this as her chance to escape.

"Thank you," she said, and reached for the *Leave Meeting* button.

"I am here if you need me," the woman said, "and in case you want further spiritual guidance, I will send you a brochure to help in your journey." She showed Melody a pamphlet with a picture of Jesus looking up at the sky and the title, *God's Answers in Time of Suffering*."

Melody said thank you again, feeling anger rather than gratitude. What did the woman mean by "why this happened to you?" No god who believed in justice would do this to an innocent child on purpose, no matter what the sins of the parents had been. This could not be payback for something either she or Emily had done.

When the brochure arrived the next day, she ripped it into fragments and neatly deposited them in a trash container, muttering "I don't think so." The Aryan Jesus with blue eyes, perfectly trimmed beard, and soulful expression no longer spoke to her.

She had better luck with talking to Mac. On his suggestion, she called Home Services to hire a physiotherapist. After a day, the one woman she hired quit, saying the risk made it "unwise" to continue.

After four days, Emily had made some progress. Her muscle strength increased enough that she could walk around the yard unassisted. She still had little appetite, but could tolerate yogurt with honey and some bland solid food.

Every day Melody talked to Mac, who reassured her that the slow recovery was still in the range of normal. "How many months do you think it will take, Mac?"

"Maybe a long time. Would you consider a rehab hospital now?"

"Yes, you were right to suggest it in the first place. I'm going crazy here trying to be nurse and physiotherapist and psychologist and every other damned health care worker. I also have to think about getting back to work. It's been four weeks now and I told my producer two. How would I find a rehab that would take someone with COVID-19?"

Mac called back a few hours later. "There is a good rehab center two miles from you. I've sent in Emily's data. They should be able to take her in three days."

"How wonderful. Thank you so much. I don't know what I'd do without you."

CHAPTER THIRTY-ONE

PAVANE

JUNE 24-26, 2020
BOSTON, MA

As a surgeon, Mac had learned to rouse from deep sleep to alertness in seconds. When he saw the caller ID on his phone at five a.m. the next morning, he answered anxiously. "Melody?"

"Mac?" Shaking sobs. "I think Emily's dead."

"Dead? What happened?"

"I woke about four because something was not right. She wasn't breathing. I called 911. The EMT's tried starting her heart but got no response. They're taking her to the hospital now. I'm driving behind them in the car."

"You did just right, Melody. Call me back as soon as you know anything more."

Her call came an hour later. "She's been officially declared dead, Mac. And we can't even have a proper burial."

"I'm so sorry."

"I want to know why she died."

"What did the doctors there say?"

"Heart stoppage. They say they can't be more precise without an autopsy, and they have no facilities for a COVID-19 autopsy. I need to know if this was from her infection."

"I'll call my CDC contact. Perhaps he can arrange a postmortem in Manhattan."

"Can you be involved as well?"

"I think so. Will you be OK?"

"Of course not."

Mac's old friend Russ Baxter at the CDC was not happy about receiving a phone call at 5:30 a.m. He was even less happy about trying to arrange for an autopsy on a COVID patient.

"Russ, this is not the usual case," Mac said. "There's something wrong about this girl's pattern. She seemed to be doing fine, then suddenly died. If this is related to coronavirus, it may mean a new strain has emerged. What I'm really worried about is that this may be ongoing infection on top of the increased immune response."

"I'll call around," Russ said, "see if I can get a postmortem set up. I can't promise anything."

As he finished his conversations, Mac realized Lauren was awake.

"Everything all right?" she asked.

"No."

"Can you talk about it?"

Usually Mac would not say anything about his patients because of HIPAA regulations. However, he simply could not keep his distress contained. While they sat on the patio with morning coffee, Mac filled Lauren in on the last stage of Emily's journey. Lauren sat without speaking.

"That's awful. I'm so sorry," she said at the end of his description. "Worse than my dad. And the problem of not saying a proper goodbye..."

A telephone ring interrupted them.

"Russ?" Mac answered.

"They'll do the autopsy at Montefiore Medical Center in the Bronx."

"Can you make sure they send tissue to my lab for analysis?"

"Goddammit, Mac, you want a lot."

"The patient's mother made a specific request. She's Melody Swift. I don't think you want to cross her."

"I have no idea who that is, but we'll get you tissue."

Two days later, Mac and his virologist Linda Watkins met with Melody via Zoom. "We've just done a viral analysis of Emily's tissues," Watkins began.

"And?" Melody asked, voice sounding desperate with fatigue and worry.

"Emily died with extensive coronavirus invasion of her heart, brain, lungs, and gut. She also had a marked inflammatory response to the virus. The most likely cause of death was an overwhelming myocarditis."

"What does that mean, Mac?" Melody asked in a plaintive tone.

"The muscles of the heart were inflamed from the virus and the heart could not beat."

"But this virus is supposed only to infect the lungs."

"That's what's so important," Watkins said. "We've done sequencing on Emily's virus. It's a new mutant form of the coronavirus. Among other things, the spike proteins are different."

"Spike proteins?" Melody asked, shaking her head.

"The hooks coronaviruses use to latch onto specific cells. You remember me telling you the way the virus works is to anchor, eat holes in the cell membrane, inject RNA, and take over the cell machinery to make new viruses. If it can't stick to a cell, it can't enter it."

"So how is Emily's virus different?"

"You asked about it when we met back in March," Mac said. "The regular coronavirus has a key to enter only some cells that line our nose and lungs. This new virus can attack everywhere."

"And so what happens? I'm so confused in my thinking now I don't remember much."

"Exactly what happened to Emily," Mac said. "This mutant virus has a master key to enter any cell in the body. It infected her heart and brain more than the lungs."

"One bright note is that the spikes on the new strain are more likely to produce antibodies than they were on the previous version of the virus," Watkins said. "It may be easier to create a vaccine to this strain."

"Can I do anything to help you right now, Melody?" Mac asked. He felt empathy and pity for a woman who he admired, even though her political leanings were so different from his.

"Yes, you can stand on the rooftops and shout that everyone should take this damned virus seriously. Oh wait, you tried that three months ago. We smart asses didn't believe you."

"I'm sorry."

"Better yet, you could get rid of those bastards who say there's nothing to worry about from this virus." She paused. "Including our fearless leader." She killed the screen image.

CHAPTER THIRTY-TWO

TURNAROUND

JUNE 26-27, 2020
GREENWICH, CT

Melody retreated to her home office. She stared at the pictures on the walls and the memorabilia on the shelves, realizing now how much the room displayed her desire for affirmation. That need had allowed her to accept and promote policies she now considered reprehensible.

The most important photographs hung on her 'wall of fame.' They included many of the luminaries of her political party and proved how successful she had been as a spokesperson for the right wing.

Virtually all the photos were personally signed to her and displayed white men older than she. As she rummaged through her utility drawer, she thought of her parents. No one could ever replace the sense of security they—especially her father—had provided in her Virginia home.

Perhaps that was why she had always gravitated to strong men, and why she felt so comfortable in their presence.

It was all upside down now. The man she had put her

ultimate trust in, the leader of her country, had betrayed her and helped kill her daughter.

She found the hammer. With narrowed eyelids, she stopped in front of each portrait. Her response today differed from her usual glow of admiration. Anger and contempt built within her as she contemplated the photographs one by one.

The first image pictured the full Republican Senate delegation standing outside the Capitol, with the president grinning at the center. Almost all were white males, and in this informal shot some of them vigorously slapped each other on the back like frat brothers.

Melody shook her head as she looked at them one by one, then shouted, "Enablers! Flunkies! Cultists! How could I go along with your lies?"

Anger built within her like a volcano, leaking lava of hate over the politicians she had once defended so vigorously. She knew that her brain was not working right, was not allowing her the control over her thoughts and actions she once felt so important in her life. But she also knew she could never again return to the deceptions of her broadcast career.

Whack!

The glass of the group photograph shattered onto the floor in thin fragments as she pulled back, hammer poised for another blow.

"You!" she pointed to the portrait of the senate majority leader. "You told me in confidence that the virus was exactly what we needed. It targeted old people, ethnic minorities, and the inner city. You actually *wanted* it to ravage those groups."

The hammer hit him right between the eyes, followed by several blows to pulverize the picture.

"And *you*!" she stopped in front of the vice-president, her pulse mounting. "You thought this was God's judgment on gays and Blacks. How do you feel now that the plague is rampaging through your supporters, devastating Christian parents and children? You continue to advocate for reopening churches even though that recommendation risks thousands of lives. How can you do that? Maybe this virus is God's judgment on you, you son-of-a-bitch, not on the groups you're so afraid of."

She began on one side and smashed the glass in sequential fragments, ignoring the blood now seeping from the lacerations on her arms. The volcano within her was in full eruption now, and she felt the heat of her hate.

"***You***!" The picture of the president holding the bible in front of a church loomed before her. "You used us Christians as tools. You manipulated us and betrayed our trust, denied what you knew to be true, and led thousands of us to slaughter. You drained my precious blood to protect your own despicable skin."

She lifted her middle finger and said with a voice trembling with rage. "You, you motherfucker, don't give a damn about anyone but yourself and the sick power base you're trying to build to get re-elected. You are the Abomination."

She ripped the picture off the wall, tearing the nail out with it, and smashed it to the floor, stomping it over and over. Her leg began to bleed where a shard of glass embedded itself. She looked at it without emotion and felt no pain as she pulled it out.

Without a glance at the shattered glass, blood, and broken frame fragments she left behind her, she stormed out of her office. She halted in front of the full-length mirror in her foyer, a mirror which she had often used to make sure she fit the image male politicians desired.

"And you!" she shouted at her own reflection. "You helped them all, acted as a mouthpiece for them, compromised your own health. Your ambition killed your daughter. You—"

Something in the image stopped her. She had a few lacerations, but that was not it. She moved closer to the mirror to confirm what she saw. The whites of her eyes were bloodshot. On her left shoulder, a multitude of red dots coalesced into a blotch two inches in diameter.

She smashed the mirror, watching her image crack, shred, and disappear. The shards fell around her as tears of fear and frustration slid down her cheeks.

She moved away from the shattered glass and sank to the floor, leaning against the far wall. *What were those shoulder spots? Why were the whites of her eyes red?*

Fear began to add to her anger. Reaching into her pocket, she pulled out her cell phone and called Mac.

"Mac, it's Melody. I just noticed I have red eyes and a skin rash."

"Is the rash swollen or itchy?"

"No. It's like hundreds of little dots."

"If you press on it, does it turn white?"

"Yes."

"Get to an emergency room."

"What do you think it is?"

"I don't know, but you need to be tested."

"For what? It can't be COVID-19 again. I've already had it, right?" Her pulse raced and hand trembled.

"It could be a recurrence."

She almost dropped the phone. "I want you to check me out."

"You should see someone faster and closer to home."

"I need someone I trust."

"You can't go anywhere by train or commercial airline. You'd have to arrange a private plane again to get up here."

"I can drive up. It's almost easier to go to Boston than to take a car into Manhattan."

"Do you feel well enough to drive?"

"I'm OK except for the skin blotches. And maybe my thinking's a little confused. But you really believe this could be COVID-19?" Her heart felt as if a giant hand squeezed it as she spoke.

"I do, and I have no idea why you would get it a second time," Mac said. "If you insist on coming here and don't want to spend the next month in the hospital, we should meet outside the hospital on the harbor front. And you would have to go back to Greenwich this afternoon."

The trip to Boston took only three hours. There was almost no traffic on the freeway, which brought her almost directly onto Seaport Boulevard. Miraculously, a car pulled out from a meter space just in front of her and she could park a block from the hospital.

Following Mac's directions, she maneuvered to a bench on the harborwalk. Although the day was stifling hot, the air still smelled fresh and cool at the water's edge. The brilliant reflection of the mid-day sun dazzled her. The buzz of activity she had come to associate with the harbor was almost back to full volume.

As she inhaled sea air through her mask, she had the paralyzing thought—*Could this be the last time I see Boston harbor?*

Mac was wearing a black N95 mask, sitting on a bench overlooking the water. He got up as she arrived and slipped on clear vinyl gloves. She described her symptoms and showed her shoulder rash.

"I want you to go to Dr. Watkins' lab for a nasal swab and blood draw."

"Aren't you going to check my temperature?"

"No."

"I'm not going into a hospital."

"That's why we're meeting here. You will have to return to Greenwich tonight. If you stay in Boston, I'm obligated to report to the department of public health that you are a likely COVID-19 case. You'll end up in a hospital whether you like it or not."

"I'll go back, I promise."

His face softened. "Will you be OK by yourself?"

"Definitely. My neighborhood's completely safe. I don't even lock the back door when I leave in the morning."

"I wasn't talking about that kind of safety. I meant will you be OK emotionally? This must be a very frightening time for you."

"I'll be fine by myself. And I don't want to be around anyone else right now. I need to be alone."

"You have my cell number. Call any time day or night if you need me," he said as he gave her the street address of Dr. Watkins' lab. "I'm sorry we can't shake hands, but I'm praying for you."

"Thanks. I am really grateful to know that, and to know you," she said, and headed back to her car.

She found the lab easily, had the blood and nasal swab taken, and got onto the Mass Turnpike before rush hour. She hardly noticed the ride back to Greenwich. After the cascade of emotions she had experienced over the day, she felt completely hung over, almost numb.

She arrived home around seven p.m. and collapsed onto the bed.

The next morning, Mac and Watkins woke her with a video call.

"We have bad news," Watkins began. "You're infected by the same virus strain that killed Emily."

"Except your virus chose to attack skin and eyes first," Mac interjected. "We assume it's also in other organs, but there's no way of knowing."

"Am I contagious?"

"Very," Watkins said. "Even though you don't have severe respiratory symptoms, the lining of your nose is loaded with the virus. You would be considered a superspreader. You shed virus with every cough, but you are not sick yourself."

"How did I get it again?"

"We think it mutated in Emily, then reinfected you," Mac said. "Like the common cold, this virus can change some of its characteristics so previous immunity doesn't work. The bad thing is that in its new version it has the master key to enter all your organs. It can infect every part of your body, and the body won't do anything to stop it."

"I actually have some symptoms I was afraid to tell you about," Melody said. "For example, I have trouble thinking straight."

"That's because your brain is infected," Mac said. "That was one of the scariest features of my COVID-19 infection. I even hallucinated for a few days."

"I also cough when I get tired and have a hard time getting enough air into my lungs. I'm exhausted. My gut is churning as if there were no tomorrow."

"This is virus in the lungs, the gut and the blood," Mac said.

"But I don't have a fever. Why is that?"

"A fever results from the body's attempt to fight the virus," Mac said. "Your body may have given up that fight."

"You mean I'm going to die soon?"

Melody could tell by the expression on Mac's face the answer was yes. She looked straight at the video camera on her computer, hoping to stare Mac into a response.

"Mac?" she asked.

Mac looked away.

"Mac, I asked you a question."

"Who can tell for sure?" he replied.

"Mac, I consider you a friend as well as a doctor," Melody said. "How long do I have?"

"Our guess is maybe two weeks," Mac said. "I'm so sorry."

CHAPTER THIRTY-THREE

HAVE YOU FORSAKEN ME?

JUNE 27-29, 2020
GREENWICH, CT

Sitting alone after the call, Melody tried to comprehend the full implications of her reinfection. She had difficulty understanding most things now. Her mind seemed confused, working half in the present and half in a world of shadows.

She wandered around her house, looking at the shards of glass and picture frames still on the floor, at Emily's room preserved as Emily had left it, at the shattered mirror in the hall.

She collected a few of Emily's possessions. A favorite teddy bear, Emily's cell phone with the heart stickers on it, a night-time reading book, a princess note pad. She placed these on her own bedside table, hoping they would keep her daughter's memory close, and sat in mourning on her bed.

The clang of her cell phone interrupted her.

"Melody Swift."

She winced at the voice.

In the past, a call from the president always made her

feel special. It was awesome to realize that she, a Virginia nobody, would get a direct call from the most powerful man in the country.

Today, she cringed. *What did he want from her now?*

"Mr. President?"

"It's time for another transfusion."

"Transfusion?"

"Yes. Your antibodies. So far, they've been doing a great job. I've never felt better."

"But—"

"No buts. Remember how many good things I've done for you. I set aside an hour in my schedule Monday. I want you to report to the White House at one o'clock. Of course, you must keep this a complete secret. It would make me look bad for people to know. Very bad."

"But Mr. President, I—".

"Don't tell me you can't arrange it. This gives you two days to prepare. And I know you're on leave from your show."

"My daughter just died."

"I've missed *Swift Currents*. Spreads my message."

"Didn't you hear me? I said my daughter just died."

"Oh. I'm sorry for your loss. You know my daughter, of course. She married a genius."

Melody narrowed her eyes and shook her head. Was this man's whole world only about him? She had always admired his conviction that he had the answer to everything. Perhaps that was the reason she had supported him without question.

But did he *ever* think about anyone else? She considered his disregard for protective measures against COVID-19, his lies about the disease, the deadly result for her and her daughter. Was it possible that he cared nothing about other people—their lives, or their deaths?

And now he placed an opportunity before her. The lying, bullying, and chaos—these could go away with one transfusion of her deadly blood. The transfusion he was demanding now.

She shuddered. *This was the president of the United States. What was she even thinking? Not only that, but intentional taking of human life was against God's law.*

"I can't do it," she said. "I have—"

"I don't care what you have. That's not the right answer."

"You caught me in the middle of something, Mr. President. I need a few minutes."

"I'm a very busy man. No one's busier than me. I'll give you ten."

He hung up.

Melody sat staring at a picture of Jesus hanging on her bedroom wall. He wore a crown of thorns, with blood and sweat dripping down his face.

When she was fourteen, that image had been the source of a spiritual experience that convinced her to adopt Christianity like a second skin.

She remembered the earnest theology of her adolescent years. "Jesus died for you, Melody," her pastor said. "He willingly staggered to his death at Golgotha to save us all."

As she stared at the picture on her wall, she considered the sense of betrayal that must have raced through Jesus' mind as he felt his life ebbing away on the cross. It was the same as the betrayal she felt right now, deep within her soul. "My God, my God, why has thou forsaken me?" Jesus had cried.

But his God, his Father, had not forsaken him. He had used him to change the world.

The image began to transform. The sun-darkened skin and unkempt beard morphed into a woman with hazel eyes and stringy auburn hair. Melody's own face looked back at her from the image, filthy, scratched, tear-stained, with blood dripping from her eyes.

With her death, she could atone for the innocent loss of life that resulted from her perpetual denial of COVID-19, her refusal to acknowledge the danger of coronavirus.

But with her blood. . .

With his precious blood, Jesus had saved the world.

With her sacred blood, she could save at least some of the world. She could prevent thousands of deaths that would surely result from continued denial of this virus.

The image stared at her, compelling her to act.

She tried to return the president's phone call as an automatic dial-back. It came up as *no caller ID*. She fumbled for the secret address book in her purse to find the right number.

She had considered it one of the great triumphs of her career when the president gave that number to her. "Only a few people in the world have this," he had said. "Do not share it with anyone and only use it if you have something really good to tell me."

She wrote the number down on Emily's pad beside her bed, then tapped it into her phone.

"Not bad. Only seven minutes," he answered.

"OK, Mr. President. I'll go ahead."

"That's my girl. I knew you'd do what I wanted. Remember, White House at one o'clock Monday. Wear something I like."

Melody wrote the time and place on the pad to make sure she remembered accurately. So much was confusing these days. She wasn't sure she could trust her own memory.

The following day, Melody fortified herself. She attended streaming church services. She prayed and she meditated. She considered the commandment not to murder and weighed it against the innocent Americans who the president had led to their deaths by his COVID-19 policies.

Emily's death tilted the balance. An eye for an eye. A life for a life.

And if he just took her blood with her consent, she wouldn't be doing anything active, just letting him have his way.

She felt scales had been lifted from her eyes, just as they had for the blind men Jesus cured. With her new vision, she saw clearly her president's repeated violations of the ten commandments: adultery, business thefts, false witness against anyone who opposed him, covetousness of anything and everything he didn't have, even the deaths of thousands who believed his lies, a kind of murder.

She contrasted the president's self-absorption with her savior's willingness to show the greatest love of all—to lay down his life for others.

She reminded herself that the stories of Jesus were stories of love, especially for the dispossessed: forgiving the prodigal son, rescuing an adulteress from stoning, eating with prostitutes and tax collectors, healing women with uncontrollable menstrual bleeding. These were tales of compassion. They stood in sharp interest to the lack of concern for the disadvantaged she saw emanating from the White House.

She considered the sycophants, including senators and Right TV colleagues, who had sold their soul. They would get their just reward. She did not care about them. She just wanted her life for a life.

Which led her back to her daughter. She again saw Emily's shy smile, felt her gentle hand as it slid into hers, remembered the scent of freshly scrubbed skin after a bath, heard the sound of her breathing at night. She wept as she rocked back and forth on her bed. Life without Emily was pointless. Death would be a blessing.

By the end of the day, she was emotionally ready for Monday. She felt that she, unlike thousands of other desolate parents, had been given the opportunity to change the world. Her God had not forsaken her. He had given her a mission.

She slept well.

CHAPTER THIRTY-FOUR

PREPARATION

MONDAY, JUNE 29, 2020
GREENWICH, CT, AND WASHINGTON, DC

On Monday morning, Melody spent the first hour trying to get her face back to the tanned, flawless look she had cultivated all her professional life. It didn't work, but she deemed herself presentable by the time she finished her makeup.

She chose a red flowered sundress with pearl necklace and earrings, and added a silk scarf to cover the rash on her shoulders. They were Emily's favorites. She shut the door on her office and living room, leaving them as disaster areas.

Just before she left the house, she called Mac. She wanted him to know she was grateful. It was eight a.m., and she thought she might catch him before work.

The call went to voicemail. The message she left was simple. "Mac, it's Melody. You were right. I hope I can take care of the problem. You've been wonderful to me and my family. Thank you for everything."

She exited by the back door, leaving it unlocked as she

always did, and set off for LaGuardia Airport and the shuttle to Washington.

She arrived at the entrance to the White House at 12:45 p.m., expecting to be shown through as easily as when she came on Right TV business.

"Name, please," the young guard asked. He was new, not the security person she had dealt with in the past. He wore a mask.

"Melody Swift. Where's George? He's usually posted here."

"He got COVID-19," the man said while he searched his computer screen. "Ms. Swift, I don't have you on my list."

"There must be some mistake. I'm to see the president at one." Melody had not anticipated this. Her heart raced. Had the president changed his mind or forgotten about this meeting?

"Not according to this schedule."

"Can you call his executive secretary?"

"I can't call his office every time someone says they have an appointment. You'll have to show me some documentation."

"But he's expecting me." She showed her press badge.

"I have no evidence of that."

"It's imperative that I see him."

"I'm going to have to ask you to leave, Ma'am."

"But—"

"Now, please." The guard put a hand on the pistol at his hip and took a step toward her.

Melody backed away, with a momentary urge to cough in his face. His mask would make that useless.

"Ms. Swift?" a voice behind the guard asked. The voice materialized into a thirty-something woman, tanned and buff, in a black suit and black mask. Her manner shouted secret service even more than her earbud.

"Yes," Melody answered, still panicked by this turn of events.

"I have orders to take you to the Oval Office. Sorry if your name wasn't on our official list. Apparently an administrative foul-up."

And a way of keeping any hard evidence I was ever here off the books, Melody thought.

"She hasn't done the COVID-19 screening," the guard protested.

The agent looked at her watch. "I'm supposed to have her at the president's door in three minutes."

She turned to Melody. "Have you had any recent cough, fevers, change of smell, foreign travel, or exposure to someone with COVID-19?"

"No," she lied.

"Check her temperature," the woman said to the guard, who aimed the temperature gun at Melody's forehead from a foot away, then glanced at the reading. "Looks fine."

"OK. We're good to go. Let's not keep the president waiting." She led Melody to the outside door of the Oval Office and told her to stand there.

The president appeared a few moments later, no mask in place. "Thanks, Jane," he said to the agent. "I'll be ten minutes. Wait for me here."

"You look terrible," he said to Melody as he led her down the corridor. He slipped a blindfold over her eyes. "I can't let you see where we're going. Keep up with me."

"Know why I look so bad? I told you yesterday. My daughter died," she called out as she tried to follow his voice, lost without visual guidance. Her pride would not allow her to put her arms out to feel her way. Several times she stumbled.

"I told you I was sorry to hear that. But you should use more makeup so people won't know. Your ratings are going to tank if you go back on TV looking like that."

She realized he had stopped when she collided with him. After a few seconds, what sounded like thick vault doors slid open. They stepped through and waited again. She heard an elevator approach. It made a lot of noise. Clearly it was not one of the modern high-speed types.

When it arrived, the president pushed against her shoulder to move her into it. She almost tripped over the unevenness of the floor as she entered.

After descending a minute and hearing the doors open, she was nudged out. She had no idea how large the space was, and she heard no sound but her own footsteps. It was cold and smelled moldy.

"My nurse will get you set up." The president's voice came from the elevator behind her.

As she heard the doors close, a cool hand touched hers. "Can I take my blindfold off now?" Melody asked.

"No. Please keep it on and climb onto the bed."

Melody recognized the voice of the same nurse who had taken her blood two months ago. It seemed more strained than the last time they met, and it was muffled, as though she spoke through a mask.

"Where are we?" Melody asked.

"I can't tell you that."

"It's the bunker, isn't it? I didn't realize it was being used again," Melody continued, remembering the uproar about the president sitting in this room during the Floyd demonstrations.

"I can't say. What's this rash?" the nurse asked, touching Melody's shoulder.

"Poison ivy. I've been scratching." Melody shrugged, adjusting her silk scarf so that it covered the area.

"It doesn't look like poison ivy to me. And you look a lot less well than you did last time. Are you sure you're not sick?"

"I had a COVID-19 test two days ago, and it was negative." She hoped God would forgive her for lying.

"I want just to check something," the nurse said, and Melody heard her move away.

Melody strained to hear the conversation. Was her plan going to be blocked at the last minute? Her mouth became dry and she could feel her pulse race.

"I'm not sure she's well," she heard the nurse say, then pause. Melody waited anxiously.

"She says she had a negative test two days ago."

"Yes, sir, Mr. President. Whatever you say. Sorry to interrupt you."

"What's happening?" Melody asked, pretending she didn't hear anything, as the nurse's footsteps returned.

"Nothing. We're going ahead as planned, but we'll take two pints of blood this time. We need your signature first."

She took Melody's hand, placed a pen in it, and guided it to a piece of paper. "It says you'll take no legal action for anything following this procedure."

Melody scribbled her initials with her right hand as the nurse prepared the other arm. She felt the hated jab as the needle penetrated her skin. The nurse taped up the IV, attached it to a board to keep her elbow straight, then moved away until Melody could no longer hear her footsteps.

If Melody lifted the corner of the blindfold, she could get a glimpse of her surroundings.

A plastic bag hung from an IV pole, filling slowly with her blood, draining her energy with each drop. She could see a partition beside her. The foot of another bed protruded behind it, presumably for the president when he got here. There was sparse illumination from ceiling lights that looked as if they were part of a large meeting room.

The nurse came in several times, expressing displeasure at the slow collection, lowering the bag to get it to fill.

Melody lay, cold and anxious, waiting for the president to appear.

CHAPTER THIRTY-FIVE

REACHING THE PRESIDENT

MONDAY, JUNE 29, 2020
BOSTON, MA, AND GREENWICH, CT

Mac was on an administrative Zoom meeting when Melody's call buzzed that Monday morning. He clicked onto her voicemail as soon as his meeting finished.

To his professional ear, it sounded like the call of a patient about to commit suicide.

She was at high risk as a mother who had just lost a child. He thought back to the thin, anxious women he had seen on Friday. Had she decided to end her life purposely rather than waiting for the ravages of the disease?

His stomach twisted. He called, texted, and emailed Melody, but got no response. He looked at his watch. Eight-forty.

He rang the Greenwich police.

"My name is Duncan MacGregor. I'm a doctor from Boston. I have reason to be concerned about a woman who lives in Greenwich named Melody Swift. She just experienced a significant loss and called me with a message that sounds like a suicide note."

"Are you her doctor?"

"One of them, yes."

"Have you tried calling our suicide help line?"

"It's not about me."

"They have suggestions about what to do. We get calls about people all the time. We don't follow them for twenty-four hours unless there's a good reason."

"I told you I'm a doctor," Mac said, "I really think you should go by the house. Here is the address. I assume this call is being recorded in case something bad has happened."

There was silence for several seconds. "We'll have a cruiser go by. Call me back in fifteen minutes."

Mac paced for twelve minutes, then called.

The same voice answered. "Our cruiser went to the house, even rang the bell. Nobody's there. The car is gone. A neighbor said she saw the woman leave about eight o'clock. I expect she's very much alive."

Mac felt relief flood his system. "Thanks for checking it out," he said, then sat staring at the phone remembering a cardinal rule of surgery—*Never rely on someone else's observations.* He tapped his fingers on the desk, walked around his office, tried to do some work. He could not leave it alone. There was something wrong with that voicemail.

He yielded to his instincts and decided to check Melody's house out for himself. At nine-fifteen he steered his car onto the Mass Pike, heading for Greenwich, Connecticut.

Monday was a research and writing day for him, without scheduled events except a lab meeting. It was the easiest day of the week to take off. From the car, he called his wife, his secretary, a surgeon to cover emergencies, and his research laboratory director, to let them know he would be out of town for a few hours.

He reached Melody's address at 12:45, half an hour later than the navigation initially predicted. He rang the doorbell, with no answer and no apparent activity in the house. Remembering Melody's comment that her neighborhood was so safe she habitually left her rear door unlocked, he circled round the back and entered without difficulty.

He gasped when he saw the smashed photographs in the office and the fractured mirror in the hall. *It looks like she's flipped from love to hate for her own leaders.*

He climbed the stairs to the second floor.

A brightly colored suite with a single bed and adjoining bathroom reminded him of his own daughter. Stickers of heroic women, fictional and real, spotted the walls. A small desk, an iPad, and earphones sat along one side of the room. A child-sized chair against the opposite wall was joined by a collection of action figures along the floor. A small bookshelf overflowed with books. The bed was meticulously made, with plush animals beside the pillow.

It looked as though Emily would be back right after school.

The master bedroom door stood partly open at the end of the hall. As Mac entered it, a picture of Jesus dominated the space: a crown of thorns on his head, eyes uplifted, face lacerated and bruised, blood dripping from his scalp.

The rest of the room was more soothing: beige rug with thick pile, king-size bed with white table on either side, large white dresser, and makeup table including mirror.

Mac glanced into the *en suite* bathroom with shower, jacuzzi tub, marble sink, and bidet toilet. Looking for Melody, he stepped into a large walk-in closet with elegant dresses on hangers, shelves containing neatly folded clothes, and racks filled with designer shoes.

Melody was nowhere to be found. However, there was evidence she had been there recently. A half-cup of cold coffee sat in front of the makeup mirror. One of the bedside tables was set up like a shrine to her daughter: a framed picture of Emily, a colorful note pad, a child's storybook of the bible, a small stuffed animal, and a cell phone with heart-shaped stickers and the stenciled name *Emily.*

The notepad displayed writing in Melody's hand.

POTUS 1 pm Monday.

Knowing that Melody was infected with a new coronavirus strain, Mac gasped at the implication of that note. His heart paused, then flipped. He felt sweat bead on his brow.

Had he gotten the point of Melody's message completely wrong? "I hope I can take care of the problem." *Was the* ***president*** *the problem? Were those smashed pictures symbolic of disaffection so severe Melody was willing to try to infect the country's leader?*

Mac, like millions of others, did not think the administration's handling of COVID-19 was sensible. But what person in her right mind would consider assassination as a solution?

That, of course, was the problem. Melody had told him she was confused. She was not in her right mind.

He could not rid himself of the idea that she planned to kill the president.

And it would be easy. In her present condition, she was as lethal as a suicide bomber. If Melody met the president face-to-face, he was at great risk.

One o'clock was five minutes away.

Mac sat on the bed sorting out his options. The count-down had begun, and time was his enemy. There was no point in calling the White House. No one would believe him, and the situation would take longer than five minutes to explain. He would not be able to connect with anyone powerful enough to stop a meeting quickly.

His CDC contact would be useless for this.

Only one name came to his mind. Several years ago, he had been introduced to CIA chief James Brogan after receiving the Presidential Citizen's Medal. He had put Brogan's personal card in his wallet. Fumbling, he found it there and reached for his cell phone.

"Damn." He realized he left his phone in the car, attached to the navigation system.

He felt his world morph into unreality. Sitting in an elegant Greenwich bedroom, he had to stop an assassination attempt that might be starting right now three hundred miles away. His pulse raced and sweat dripped into his eyes.

He picked up the cell phone marked *Emily* from the bed-side table. It unlocked without a code and was powered up.

Brogan answered on the third ring.

"Mr. Brogan, this is Duncan MacGregor. I—"

"I remember you, Dr. McGregor. Good to hear from. I hope you've been well."

"I've been fine. I have an urgent problem—"

"I should tell you I left the CIA a month after the new administration was sworn in," Brogan said. "I don't have anything official to do with the agency now."

"I don't know who else to turn to. I think there may be an attempt on the president's life happening right now."

Mac explained the background and the problem. "So, how can I warn the president? Can you find out if there is a woman named Melody Swift on his schedule today? Is he with her right now, when all this is supposed to be happening?"

"I still have some contacts. I'll work on it. Stay beside your phone."

Five minutes later, he called Mac back. "No Melody Swift on the office schedule, and the president is supposed to be in the office for the next hour. In fact, he just left for twenty minutes to practice golf swings. He does that a lot. Maybe you have the wrong day. My source checked for the entire week and says there's no one with the name Swift listed."

"Thanks, Jim." Mac sat stunned. *Had his instincts misled him?* He picked up the notepad from the bedside table and flicked through it as he considered what to do.

A telephone number leaped out from the third page.

He stared at it for a few seconds, then picked up Emily's phone and tapped in the number.

"Who the hell is this?" a voice answered. Mac thought he heard an elevator close in the background, but he mainly paid attention to the voice. He had heard it a thousand times.

"Mr. President, I—"

"Whoever you are, I'll track you down. No one gets this number." The connection severed.

Mac called back. The phone rang three times, then connected.

Mac said as fast as he could, "If-you're-meeting-Melody-Swift-today-you-should-know-she's-reinfected-with-a-very-aggressive-coronavirus."

The line went dead.

He tried again, but the call went directly to voicemail.

Mac hung up and sat stunned.

Melody had a direct line to the president. Not surprising.

But what had just happened? Had the president heard what he said? Had Mac successfully warned the president of the United States that he faced an assassination attempt more deadly than a sniper's bullet?

Or was the whole thing his wild fantasy? Perhaps Melody would walk through the door in the next minute and ask what he was doing there.

The cell phone's ring tone jarred him.

It was Brogan. "MacGregor," he said, "I don't know what hornet's nest you've stirred up or where the hell you are, but get out of there fast. Wipe anything you've touched. And lose the phone. They're tracking its GPS." He hung up.

Mac got up with heart hammering. He used disinfectant wipes from the master bathroom on everything he had come in contact with, but took the notepad and cell phone with him. He raced for the car, estimating he was out the door three minutes after Brogan called.

He drove away, meticulously staying under the speed limit.

Two unmarked black vehicles with sirens screaming headed past him toward the house as he turned the corner.

He pulled into a gas station just before the highway and parked. He smashed Emily's phone under his heel, and dumped it into a sewer.

Back on the road, he merged with a line of cars heading for the freeway. His heart was still pounding and his hands sweated on the wheel. He proceeded at the snail's pace of afternoon traffic, wondering whether a cardiac arrest would catch him before the police did.

Just after he entered the freeway, he saw and heard a helicopter whirl into the area he had just left. The letters FBI were emblazoned on its underbelly.

CHAPTER THIRTY- SIX

IT IS FINISHED

MONDAY, JUNE 29, 2020
WASHINGTON, DC

Melody heard the elevator door open, followed by the familiar step of the man she had come to eliminate.

At last, she thought, closing her eyes. She imagined him lying on the other side of the partition receiving her blood. Millions of viruses would course through his body to infect and destroy his organs, just as they were destroying hers. Her daughter would be avenged.

A phone rang and she heard the president speak, then stop. The phone rang again but she heard no conversation. His steps came toward her fast, with heavy breathing, as if he were building up to say something. She had the sense of great anger advancing toward her.

Then the steps stopped, as if their owner had a new thought. They hesitated for several seconds and turned the other way, with the nurse's lighter tread now accompanying them back to the elevator.

Melody strained to hear the conversation, but could make out only muffled words. She thought perhaps she heard the nurse say, "of course, I understand." The elevator doors closed, and Melody could hear it start its ascent. There were no further presidential footfalls. She and the nurse were again alone.

The nurse's steps came closer, stopping just beside Melody's bed. "We've had a change of plan," the nurse said. "The president won't take the transfusion today."

Surprise morphed into disbelief, then anger, in Melody's brain. "What do you mean he won't take the transfusion? What's wrong? What happened?"

"His schedule changed."

"Why? How? I came all this way and, and—"

"He's the president. He has a right to change his mind whenever he wants."

"Will he take it later?" Melody asked, now desperate to have some idea whether her plan would ultimately work.

"We'll hold onto your blood so he can. We're not going to give it back like we did the last time."

"You mean I went through all this for nothing?" She could not even begin to describe her emotions: surprise, confusion, uncertainty, anger. . .

If this didn't work, she would attack him in a different way. On her show, describe how he forced her give blood, repeat some of the things he and his followers had said to her, demonstrate what an unreliable, tyrannical, narcissistic bastard he was.

"I don't know whether it's for nothing," the nurse broke into her thoughts. "I don't speak for him. However, I'm worried about your blood loss. Two units is significant, and you don't look as though you have a lot to spare right now. We'd like you to stay at the Washington Towers for the rest of the day to get your strength back."

"I don't want to stay anywhere," Melody said. "I'm going home." She swung around and stepped down from the bed.

Her head spun and she felt herself falling to the floor.

Her next sensation was the nurse pressing a cold wet cloth against her forehead and holding a fractured capsule of something under her nose. It smelled strong, acrid and unpleasant, and she pulled her head back from it and flicked her eyes open.

"What is that stuff? What happened?" she asked.

"It's ammonia," the nurse said. "Ancient but effective antidote to a faint. What happened? Simple. You fainted. Got up too fast. You're in no condition to go anywhere."

She checked Melody's pulse, then helped her back onto the bed. "Drink this." Melody felt a carton pressed into her hand and drank the fluid through the straw. It was orange juice, sweet and cold.

"I'm also going to give you a liter of fluid in the IV. Why don't you rest for a little while?"

Exhausted, frustrated, and nauseated, Melody lay back on the stretcher and dozed off.

She woke up to the nurse's touch on her shoulder. "Time to go."

"How long was I asleep?" Melody asked.

"An hour. Enough time for your intravenous fluid to be absorbed. You should have enough blood volume now to walk. We've arranged for an escort to take you to the hotel, and she's waiting upstairs now."

"I told you I don't want to go to the hotel."

"What if you faint in the airport? You really need a little time to stabilize."

"I'm definitely not going to stay overnight."

"That's up to you. The hotel is run by the president's family, so he can make sure you get whatever you need. We've made the arrangements for your stay using your Right TV account. I'll take you upstairs."

A few minutes later, Melody put one hand on the nurse's shoulder and followed her to the elevator. They rode up to their destination, then walked for a short distance. The nurse removed the blindfold.

They were just inside the employee's entrance. Melody noted that some staff did not wear face masks, although the nurse wore one.

"I know where I am. I can get to the hotel alone," Melody said. "I don't need any help."

The nurse shook her head. "No way. We've arranged for Jane to escort you. And here she is." They stepped outside the door to a black Lincoln town car.

"I'm Jane," the young woman said as she opened the rear door of the car. "You OK to ride?"

Melody recognized Jane as the secret service agent who had taken her from the security desk to the president's office. She had added black leather driving gloves to her uniform.

"I'm fine," Melody said. "Sorry to waste your time with this job."

She tried to make conversation on the way to the hotel. "Were you military before secret service?"

"Yeah. Afghanistan. A lot of bad memories." Melody could see obsidian eyes staring back through the rear-view mirror.

"Glad you got back safely."

"Yeah."

At the hotel, the reception clerk welcomed Melody, asked her the usual COVID-19 questions, and gave her the key.

She couldn't get to the room fast enough. Despite her claim about being fine, she felt completely drained. Even the exertion of walking from the limousine to the hotel had made her heart race. She decided that she would stay the night after all.

She heard a knock at the door, opened it with the security chain on, and saw Jane standing there.

"Can I ask you a question?" Jane asked.

"Sure," Melody said. "Come on in." She opened the door wide and walked back toward an armchair.

She felt strong hands grab her by both shoulders and push her face down onto the bed as the door slammed shut. She twisted onto her back. A pillow pressed toward her face. She saw Jane's steel-hard eyes over the edge of the pillow before it blocked her vision.

She kicked and thrashed, twisting to free herself and get a breath. She realized that, even at her best, she was no match for the muscular body that climbed onto on her frame and pinned her to the mattress. And she was far from her best.

Melody tried to call out, but the foam of the pillow filled her mouth. She couldn't take a breath in or let one out. Panicked, she pounded the unyielding arms and torso that held her immobile.

She could feel her arms and legs weaken, could see only darkness even when she opened her eyes. As she faded, she thought she saw a ghostly Emily running towards her from the distance. The darkness suffocated her, and she saw, felt, and heard nothing.

Mac heard about Melody's death while watching the late news on CNN that evening. According to the reporter, she had been pronounced DOA at George Washington Hospital after a presumed cardiac arrest. There was no mention of a visit to the White House or other reason for her being in Washington.

He watched the bio—early television reporting for CNN, and present position as host of her own program on Right TV—then surfed other channels to find further information. He found nothing more.

He flicked off the remote and sat stunned and saddened. He knew that, with coronavirus invading her heart, Melody was a setup for a cardiac arrest. Had fate decided to cut her life short before she could implement her plan to infect the president?

But why had she been in Washington, and where had she been found? Has she met with the president? Would he show signs of infection in the next few days? Would he infect those around him?

Jim Brogan proposed an answer a few days later. His sources in the president's office told him Melody had not been seen in the White House for many weeks. They also told him to stop asking questions.

The president remained without symptoms of COVID-19.

Brogan tracked down the security guard who had been on duty the day Melody died. That guard had been fired. When Brogan had a preliminary conversation with him, he said he remembered someone with Melody's name and description. Two days later, trying to get further details, Brogan found him unwilling to say anything.

Brogan's firm conclusion was that Melody did have a scheduled clandestine meeting with the president, that Mac's call arrived in time, and that the meeting was aborted.

Mac had in fact saved the president's life.

Sitting in his study that evening, Mac could not get Melody out of his mind. He remembered the confident host of his Right TV interview, the reluctant student of the COVID-19 education session, the defiant reporter in the Bronx hospital, the despairing mother who sat by her infected daughter for weeks and found her dead, the thin, anxious woman dying from the same virus that took her daughter's life.

He felt the tragedy of Melody, and Emily, his father-in-law, and thousands of others killed by a virus whose ravages might have been lessened. Sadness overwhelmed him. Mac wept.

EPILOGUE

WEDNESDAY, DECEMBER 30, 2020
GREENWICH, CT

A year after his experience in Wuhan, Mac visited the Greenwich chapel columbarium to pay his respects to Melody and Emily Swift.

By then, more than 275,000 Americans had died from COVID-19. They were silent witnesses to the denial of coronavirus as a problem. Inadequate initial testing, incomplete containment measures, blame-shifting, lack of protective equipment, falsification of data, and rejection of scientific advice characterized this denial.

In November, Americans voted the president responsible for these policies out of office. Their vote was a reaction against an economy in disarray, hospitals filling with a new wave of COVID-19 infections, and loved ones still succumbing to the virus.

The new administration promised to listen to scientists and learn from other countries to control the outbreak.

Mac thought back to the prehistoric skulls he had seen in the Hubei museum. The brain structures that *Homo sapiens* developed 60,000 years ago to conquer enemies, could also work in the year 2020. Frontal lobes, allowing collaboration, science, and strategy, could defeat the coronavirus. The country just had to give them a chance.

Shaking his head, Mac turned to leave the memorial as his cell phone rang. He stepped outside to take the call.

"Dr. MacGregor, Jim Brogan here."

"Nice to hear from you."

"The Swift case created quite a stir. FBI, Homeland Security, even the CIA got involved. They never found out who made that call. I don't expect the former president will ever know who saved his life."

"Please don't tell him."

"Don't worry. We at the agency know and are grateful."

His tone changed from personal to professional. "I say *we* because I'm back in the CIA. And you started that ball rolling."

"What great news! Congratulations!"

"Thanks. It brings me to the real reason for contacting you today. I hope you're still willing to honor your promise to help us out from time to time."

"Of course."

"Can you meet with me this afternoon?"

"This afternoon? I'm not in Boston at the moment."

"I know. I'll come to you. We have a problem, and I need you in Africa by the end of the week."

The End

ACKNOWLEDGMENTS

I am grateful to Carole Holladay, Dorian Mintzer, Susan and Christopher Black, and my writing group (Judy and Hans Copek, Jay Shepherd, Shelly Dickson Carr, Paula Steffen, Carol Lynn, Cheryl Malone, and Stephanie McPerson) for their input at various stages of the manuscript.

Mayapriya Long of Bookwrights created the design with consummate skill and patience. The folks at Skean Dhu Press were helpful as always.

Above all, however, this book is dedicated to those affected by COVID-19, especially front-line workers who are carrying us through the pandemic. Thank you more than I can say for your dedication and heroic work.

Boston, MA
December 2020

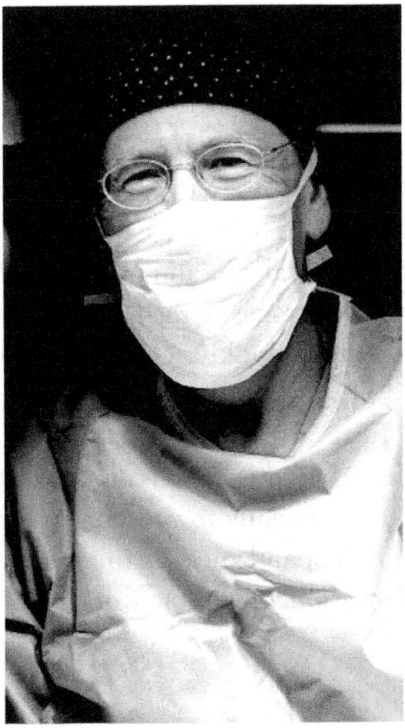

DR. PETER BLACK has served as a physician to Congress, professor of neurosurgery at Harvard, and president of the World Federation of Neurosurgical Societies. As an academic neurosurgeon, he has written a dozen books, authored hundreds of professional papers, and formed lasting friendships across the globe.

Dr. Black now writes medical fiction from his home in the greater Boston area. *Death by Denial* is his second Duncan MacGregor thriller. Be sure to read *Seizure*, his first.

You can find him on the web at peterblackbooks.com.

Made in the USA
Middletown, DE
08 November 2021

51563574R00136